HL710L

# DARK ROADS

## BLOODLINE

DANA AROS

EPIC
Press

# Bloodline
## Dark Roads: Book #2

Written by Dana Aros

Copyright © 2017 by Abdo Consulting Group, Inc.

Published by EPIC Press™
PO Box 398166
Minneapolis, MN 55439

Cover design by Candice Keimig and Kali VanZuilen
Images for cover art obtained from iStockPhoto.com
Edited by Ryan Hume

LIBRARY OF CONGRESS CATALOGING-IN-PUBLICATION DATA

Names: Aros, Dana, author.
Title: Bloodline / by Dana Aros.
Description: Minneapolis, MN : EPIC Press, [2017] | Series: Dark roads
Summary: In this map-your-destiny book, you make the decisions as John Carlos Garcia, a boy
    who suffers depression to the point of self-harm, because he must keep his sexuality a secret.
    No one knows your secret except Isaac, your boyfriend. You must reconcile who you are
    with your religious beliefs, all while trying to survive in a community and a family who see
    homosexuality as a sin.
Identifiers: LCCN 2015959189 | ISBN 9781680762617 (lib. bdg.) |
    ISBN 9781680762754 (ebook)
Subjects: LCSH: Mental illness—Fiction. | Self-injurious behavior—Fiction. | Self-destructive
    behavior—Fiction. | Suicidal behavior—Fiction. | Homosexuality—Fiction. | Gays—
    Fiction. | Identity—Fiction. | Family life—Fiction. | Interpersonal relations—Fiction. |
    Young adult fiction.
Classification: DDC [Fic]—dc23
LC record available at http://lccn.loc.gov/2015959189

*For Granny, Papa Schmidt, Grandma Vicki,*
*Papa Joe, and everyone else who taught me*
*so much about love and family*

# 1

"**D**on't think about him," you whisper to yourself. "*No pienses en el.*"

Isaac would say the Spanish sounds more poetic, soft and silent, just like when you kiss. He'd probably tell you to say it again with that stupid fucking grin on his face.

You're lying in your bed, staring at a brown stain on the ceiling. You smile, then repeat, "*No—*" A car honks outside, making you jump. You pull your hands out from behind your head and look out at the dumpsters on the other side of the street, spilling onto the sidewalks outside of Tierra Apartments. You have to stop talking to yourself. It's too dangerous.

But how can you not think about him? His name kept popping up today—breakfast, church, all day in your room while you read for school—stuck in your head like a song: *Isaac.*

"Leviticus 20:13." It's a stronger phrase—cuts against your ears, makes the other shy away.

Your apartment door squeaks open and closed in the front room, followed by your mom's light footsteps across the carpet. Midnight. She's off work, probably with employee-discounted groceries. She mutters something in Spanish but you can't make it out—you almost never can.

Something hits your window, making a light *tunk* sound. You grin and sit up in bed, pushing your hair behind your ears. You pull your shoes on. *Isaac.*

"Juan!" your mother yells from the living room. "*Estas aqui?*" She asks you this in Spanish, because, "*No quiero que pierda su patrimonio.* I don't want you to lose your heritage." Everyone speaks Spanish in Escondido—maybe even in all of SoCal—and everyone pretends they don't because *immigrant* is a bad word and *Mexican* is even worse. Two years ago, your dad gave her the Spanish-to-English dictionary he used to carry around with him. Now it just sits in the living room on the family altar table like some religious artifact, protected by the wall of crucifixes next to the TV.

You throw the blankets off and go to your window. You pop the screen out using your pocketknife—the one your dad gave you when you were twelve, with the inscription J. C. G. for John Carlos Garcia. You pull yourself over the side and gently put the screen back so it looks closed. Isaac stands across the street with some rocks in his hand, just out of the streetlight, but his hair—dyed blonde—stands out anyway under his dark hood.

He walks on one side of the street and you walk on the other. You start whistling the theme from *Jaws*, which to your satisfaction makes him laugh— you see his smile even in the dark. He puts his hands in the pockets of his jeans and skips around the first corner. Stifling a smile, you flip him off as you follow.

You pass through Clark Street downtown, trying to ignore the stupid shit he's doing to get you to laugh, through the three blocks to the park. You look for people more than cars, before crossing the street toward the moonlight reflecting off the playground structures. If anyone sees you together, it's over—and you're not sure you could survive something like that.

Once you reach him you're okay, but crossing the street makes you nervous. You hear the low, smooth sound of cars from behind the freeway wall next to the park. Before you're even halfway there, he says, "'Ey, esse," in his best *vato* voice. "Got the stuff?"

You smile, looking down at the cross on his necklace. You can breathe again and the cars seem far away. "Shut up." You push him with your shoulder. He pulls his hand out of his pocket and reaches for yours. "Not yet," you say, and he drops it.

"You're such a baby."

You pull the wire up from the bottom of the park fence. Isaac passes through first. You're about to kick it back in place when you see a figure step around the swings and behind the public bathroom. Whoever he was, he looked like he could have been your age.

"You coming?" Isaac asks.

Gently, you put the fence back down. If you bring it up now Isaac will give you a lecture about being paranoid. You have to breathe deeply and get your mind away from the mode it's in when you're talking to your parents, people at school, your neighbors, your teachers, your priest—anyone but Isaac.

You follow the dark outline of his shoulders down into the trees. When you're with Isaac, there's no label for the state of mind you fall into. For the most part, you're yourself.

Yours and Isaac's spot is a tiny area of grass surrounded by trees, just past the freeway bridge. When you look up, you can see the sky. The red-and-white light of a plane moves slowly across the clouds, and you almost have to laugh at yourself when you wonder if they can see you.

Suddenly Isaac's hands come out of his pockets and hold your neck. He puts his mouth on yours before you can pull away. You take a step back.

"Can't I give you an early happy birthday?"

You nod.

"Happy early birthday," he says and comes toward you again, kissing you harder. All the usual feelings come crashing in, the ones that come in every time just as harsh as the last. The main one, as usual, is that you wish it didn't feel so fucking good.

*No pienses en Isaac.*

When you finally release each other, Isaac looks at you carefully. Even when you can tell he's going to say something you don't like, you have to grin at the smile in his green eyes.

"I know we said not even friends in our 'real' life." He rolls his eyes as he puts air quotes around the word, *real.* Your grin disappears and you turn away from him, pulling down on your neck with both of your hands. He speaks louder. "But I was thinking we could go to Mariana's party for your birthday. We can walk in separately, and, I don't know, accidentally, drunkenly meet?"

You shake your head when you look back at him. "We've been through this before. Besides, my dad—" Your dad wants you to have a family dinner at your aunt's house for your eighteenth birthday and, as usual, bring a girlfriend so your aunt doesn't have a heart attack thinking you'll never have kids for being so shy.

"Okay, I know, I know. Forget it." He kicks at the dirt with his shoe. You brace for the truth to destroy the fragile system of lies that keeps your entire life together. Every time someone believes you, the guilt knocks you upside the head with a hammer. "Hey, can we meet up later? There's a new diner downtown—"

"Will you stop for half a second, please?" You don't want to lie to him. You don't want to make up an excuse.

He rolls his eyes. "Come on, Jay. I'm asking to

hang out with you not fuck you in front of your parents."

You shake your head and rub your eyes with your fingers, but he grabs your wrist and holds it out, turning it to show the two-inch cut, still red and thick enough to leave a scab, running alongside your vein.

"What the fuck, man. What's this?" You yank your hand back, fight off the familiar feeling of needing to defend yourself at every moment, to keep up the balancing act. This is Isaac. He's not mad; he's just hurt you can't talk to him about everything the way he can with you.

"It's nothing. I had a bad night."

"I thought you said I made you happy enough that you wouldn't have to do that anymore. You remember saying that?"

"You do make me happy," you say, avoiding his eyes. "It's just, last night—"

"Remember what you promised in January? About your birthday?"

"I remember us wanting to meet for a date tonight, not a fucking interrogation."

He steps closer and meets your eyes, sending relief through you that he doesn't walk away from you for getting mad. "You were going to come out to your parents by the time your birthday came around. It'll help you stop, okay? You'll be happier if you just—" He makes a motion with his hands. "Get it out. That's how it happened for me."

You shake your head. Of course you remember promising that. You remember being drunk when you said it too. "Can we stop talking about it?"

He turns away from you suddenly. "Fine. Just know that every secret comes out eventually. It's just a matter of when."

He sits against the base of one of the trees and tears some grass apart with his fingers. You try to stop thinking, being suspicious of everyone, scared of everything. You push hard against the cut on your wrist with two fingers. Isaac wouldn't do anything to betray your trust, no matter how badly he wants you to come out.

"What happened last night?" he asks.

You look up into the trees, avoiding Isaac's eyes. "My parents were talking about money. It was stupid."

"No offense, but everyone on Clark Street does that."

"Yeah."

"Well?"

"Nothing, really. We might not have the money for college. They were trying not to yell at each other all night in case the neighbors hear," you say. It's not really a lie, not technically.

He sighs and leans back, looking up at the sky. "There's a healthy hetero relationship, right?"

"You really don't know when to shut your mouth, do you?"

"It's got me where I am today."

You roll your eyes. "It gets you into fights. Remember Lucy?" Lucy is short for Lucero. It should make him seem less intimidating, his name, but it does the opposite. He hasn't let up for a single day since Isaac came out at the end of freshman year.

Isaac's smile disappears. "I don't want to talk about him."

You know his family from church. Your parents used to try to talk Lucy's mom out of her pill addiction with scripture, like that would help. No one will tell you what happened to them except that Lucy lives with his grandmother now. "That's not very Catholic of you."

He smiles and you know where this is going. You led him there on purpose because he's the only person you can ask without being lectured at.

"Do you believe in God?" he asks.

You smile, squinting. "Should I?" You've had this conversation before. It's more like an inside joke now; the lines are scripted.

You talk until the sky gets lighter, slipping back into your usual topic—your life, later. You want to go to the same college and live together, somewhere far away, like New York, but it seems impossible.

"Forget about the money, Jay—and the future. All I want is to be with you right now," Isaac says. He puts his head on your shoulder.

"*Te quiero*."

"*Te amo*."

When the moon falls between the branches, you finally say it. "I don't deserve you." You shake your head, trying not to speak too loud, like your voice is an inconvenience to him. "I don't deserve this."

He grabs your hands and forces you to look at him. "*Te amo*, Jay."

You nod and lean your head on his shoulder now—you'll never be able to explain it to him, your gratitude that your best friend more than just puts up with you, but loves you, let's you love him—before whispering it back, "*Te amo*," guilty, like a confession.

Once the sky gets light, the sun rises, and it's time to go. He tries to kiss you goodbye but you stop him. It's too close to daybreak and he knows it. You back away from each other and he salutes you before walking down the hill to school early. You turn and head back under the fence and toward home again so your parents see you come out of your room.

You're about to crawl back through your bedroom window from the breezeway when you hear your dad's voice behind you. He must have been called in early to work. Way early. Or maybe you were just careless and it got late again.

"John, what are you doing out?"

You throat catches. He might have seen you already. Anyone could have. That shadow. "I'm taking a run," you say.

"In jeans?"

"Yes, sir."

Sarah, a girl in her late twenties who still can't seem to graduate from UCLA, sticks her head out the window above yours. "Would you mind keeping it down, Mr. Garcia? I have a test tomorrow."

She nods and pulls herself back in when he waves to her. You face him without looking at him, wondering who else is listening. These apartments have paper walls.

He looks back at you and crosses his arms. "Your mother's inside asleep. Do me a favor and don't wake her up this time."

"Yes, sir." You nod, about to make a show of heading around the corner to the front door, but he steps close to you. You can smell his aftershave on his round face. His eyes are wide awake, a light brown that makes you feel like you could see right through him. Once a week, he gets your mom to cut his hair close.

You're nothing like him. When you look in the mirror you see long hair and tired black eyes. You're tall but scrawny. He could crush you with one arm.

"One more thing," he says so low you have to lean in closer to him and the smell of his off-brand cologne. "Your mom and I have talked about what happened the other night. We're sorry we yelled at you. Don't worry about the money. You just focus on school."

You nod.

"Understand what I'm saying? We don't need to go telling all your little friends, *comprende?*" He looks up at Sarah's window for emphasis.

"Yeah." You grab your wrist again, digging your thumbnail into the sensitive part under the sleeve of your jacket. "I know."

He yanks your wrist away. "And stop doing that. It makes you look nervous."

He takes one last look at your baggy jeans before getting in the beat-up Toyota parked on the street.

"Have a good run."

You give him a brief wave as he drives away and wait until he turns the corner to go back in through the window. It's faster this way, and quieter.

You're about to put one leg in when Mr. Alfaro opens his door, three away from yours, and shuffles out in his checkered robe to water his plants. He waves at you so you try to smile. You wait for him to close the door before dropping back into your room and back onto your bed with your arms spread wide. It's only a matter of time, Isaac said.

You look across at your hand, the veins in your wrist under your dark skin, the line. You see your tendons move when you flex it into a fist.

There are only two ways you know how to stop over-thinking everything. The first is Isaac—you can feel yourself healing when you're with him; you can feel yourself trying to be more honest and working on feeling better. But you can't always be with him. When you get home, you have to use the second way.

You don't know what it is about cutting that makes you feel so—not *good* exactly, but relieved. It's like you've been holding everything in for so long and you need somewhere to let it out, let yourself breathe. When you dig that knife into your thigh or your shoulder, your upper arms or your ribcage, you close your eyes and feel release. You focus on the knife, really feel it twisting under your skin, digging the end of the metal deep in your muscle until you feel like you're going to shout from the pain. Then you pull back, the feeling fades off, and you open your eyes. You're back in your room, under the covers, unable to see anything in the dark.

Every cut is different. Each one has its own personality: short, long, surface or a deep point. Yesterday, you slanted the blade down one way and sliced hard, then did the same on the opposite side, backwards, which was tricky. A chunk came off, but it wasn't very big, even though it bled a lot and made your whole arm feel bruised.

You pull out the knife and twirl it in your fingertips, looking at the ceiling because anywhere else will make you want to draw blood and you know you have to stop—you have to. On your wall by the door is a wooden crucifix the size of your head that your mom put there when you were little. It's from her mother's mother. You never light the prayer candles your priest, Father Mathus, gives out every year. You keep a few of the Virgin Mary ones lined up along the carpeted floor under the cross and shove the rest in a drawer. You have to stop. Jesus would want you to stop, right?

For some reason, everyone has been worse on Isaac this past week, even people from school you'd never think would whisper comments or laugh when he walks past them. Your conversations have felt stinted as your birthday gets closer, with him nagging you more than ever to tell everyone the truth and you keeping quiet, making sure your jacket covers the full length of your arms. No matter how many arguments he comes up with, you can't seem to make telling your parents now sound better than telling them before you go to college or, better yet, not telling them at all. Isaac starts tucking the cross on his neck into his shirt when he sees you. Maybe he's trying to motivate you. Or maybe it's not about you at all.

You don't need to cut yourself. You have to stop.

Leviticus 20:13 says, "If a man also lie with mankind, as he lieth with a woman, both of them have committed an abomination: they shall surely be put to death; their blood shall be upon them."

It feels right. It feels true enough so you repeat it like a prayer when you wake up and when you go to sleep, in your head this time, in case your neighbors hear you muttering to yourself and have a talk with your dad about you. You sit up and keep a towel on the cuts, turning over Leviticus 20:13 in your mind so you don't accidentally pass out and stain your mom's sheets with the blood. Next time you won't need to. Next time you'll stop—just not yet.

You don't even have to memorize it. It's like the words were always there.

They shall surely be put to death.

To come out to your parents, turn to page 24.

To keep it a secret, turn to page 31.

# 2

YOU WAKE UP SATURDAY MORNING WITH THE SUN IN YOUR EYES. Don't focus on the fact that you're coming out— don't think, don't feel, don't care if you're ready—just speak. Today, you strip away your second self.

You grab a pair of dirty jeans from the floor— since you only have two pairs they're almost never clean—and pull out your pocketknife from your drawer, flipping the blade open at the same time. You hold it against your shoulder so a t-shirt can cover it, but you pull back and fold the blade back in—maybe later. For now, you're trying to make the right choices.

You shuffle through your shirts and pull a black

one over your head before opening your bedroom door.

"*Buenos dias!*" Your mother bustles toward you with her arms out. Your dad's sitting at the table, messing with his cheap phone. The words snap you awake again. Everything feels too normal. The smell of eggs makes everything too sharp.

You open your mouth and realize you forgot to think if you should say it first in Spanish or English. "I have something to say. It's important."

You feel your breath come out tighter, something hard balls up in your stomach. Your dad's eyebrows are turned down as he squints, holding the phone far away from his face to see the screen better. You're leading yourself in the wrong direction, trapping yourself.

"Breakfast first," your mom says. "I make your favorite."

You take a deep breath. You're bridging the gap between who you are and who you want to be. There can't be two of you anymore. You know this.

Again, you feel that sense of urgency, just behind your tongue. This is the beginning of a new start.

"I've been keeping something in for a long time," you say, checking that your mom is following your English, although she's busy with the food and doesn't look at you. "*Es importante*. Please."

"What? Say it," your dad says. He hadn't spoken yet and he's still fiddling with his phone. His voice makes you stutter, but your mind is already reeling toward the truth.

"I'm trying to tell you that I'm . . . "

They both look up at you, now that you want them to look away. You should wait.

"I'm not like you guys," you finish.

"What does that mean?" your dad asks, looking at his phone again.

"I mean, I'm different. I don't know. I can't explain it." Why can't you just say one word? Gay, *joto*, homosexual, whatever. You're only making things worse. You look at the floor now, wanting to disappear. You squeeze your wrist and close your eyes. "I just haven't been feeling so good and it's because I feel like I can't tell anyone who I really am, even if I tried."

Your dad stands up, towering over you. "Just spit it out."

You're not sure how else to put it that will ease them into it. There're no bible verses you can quote that will help them understand.

You dig your nails into your skin until it feels like it draws blood. "I'm gay." Your voice sounds totally off. Your skin crawls and your shoulders shrink toward your ears, bracing for the truth to crush you. You can't even open your eyes until he speaks.

"Excuse me?" your dad says. He sets his phone down gently on the table.

"No, no. Don't listen. Come have breakfast," your mom says. Does she know? She only hears what she wants to hear.

"What did he say?"

"I said I'm gay." You thought you would feel free, but you feel more like a traitor than you ever did before. You have to save yourself, backtrack, slow down. "I mean, I don't know. I can't explain it right now."

Your dad takes a step toward you, making you shut your mouth and look up at him. For the first time you feel like you've said something that affects him, stung him—you've never been strong enough to get under his skin before. Your mom starts speaking quickly under her breath in Spanish but you can't make it out. She won't leave the food alone.

"You're a fucking—" He can't seem to finish it.

"I'm sorry."

"You want forgiveness, do you?" he says. "About what? Say it again."

You open your mouth but he shakes you by the collar of your shirt. Even the sound of your own voice would scare you.

"Say it again and you're out of this house, you hear me?"

"You can't do that," you say.

Your mom puts her hands on her face but is

looking down, like she can drown out the situation by staring at the floor. Your dad walks over to the door, but doesn't open it. People could hear.

"Get out of my house," he says. "There's no sin in the Garcia family. No stain on our bloodline."

"No, no, no." Your mom finally steps in and a part of you could hug her for giving you even that one word against him. "He doesn't need to go on the street, Pablo, he needs to find God. He will find Him again. *Por favor.*"

"I don't care where he goes." He points at you and looks down at your shirt, not meeting your eyes. "I expect you gone when I wake up tomorrow."

"Mom?"

She looks flustered. "You've sinned."

You don't know how to answer her or if it was even meant to be a question. "I don't know."

She looks up at your dad, touching his arm. "See, he can learn. He will learn."

"How?" The question surprises you with how honestly you want to know the answer. If you suffer for your sins, you'll be freed of them—that's what you've been taught. Maybe you were always meant to come out and confess so you can be forgiven. Maybe this is why you came out all along.

"You will repent," your dad says, his eyes all over you, like he could find some kind of evidence of what he's missed for so long. "If you don't, you've got no place here."

"Father Mathus. I'll call him," your mom says, leaving your dad and you alone while she walks into the bedroom.

To let them kick you out, turn to page 41.

To meet with Father Mathus, turn to page 51.

# 3

I'S BEEN A WEEK OF WAITING. PEOPLE AT SCHOOL ALREADY CALL YOU A fag because your hair is too long for a straight guy. Your shirt is too clean for a straight guy. You don't use Spanish enough for a straight guy. You use it too much for a straight guy. Ever since you and Isaac started dating in secret, you get smaller and smaller—enough to disappear.

Something must have happened because the comments are getting worse. Lucy shoves you into Isaac on the way out of the classroom. His girlfriend, Mariana, laughing by his side, sneers, "*Jotos.*"

Isaac looks at you before Lucy shoves him to the ground.

Once they pass the tree line to the quad, you ask, "Was he talking to me? Why would he say that to me?" Isaac shakes his head, brushing off his pants. "What?" you ask.

He won't look you in the eye. "I'm used to it."

---

That Sunday morning, it's really hard to stop. You want to dig deeper into your shoulder until you stop thinking that Isaac told everyone about you because he was fed up with waiting. You know the signs of lying. You're an expert. It makes sense anyway— he needs you to be with him completely, because right now, you're not enough. But you don't know how to ask him or prove it. All you have is a knife. Maybe you're just paranoid, but your thoughts won't stop spinning.

Your dad bangs his fist on your bedroom door.

"We're leaving now," he says. "Hurry up."

You reach under your bed for a towel to wipe the

blood off. Since you don't have any bandages you tear off a piece of duct tape with your teeth and stick it to your shoulder with tissues underneath. Hopefully no blood will leak onto your pale blue church shirt. Your hair should help cover the bulge.

You change, check twice that your shoulders are totally covered, and walk into the living room, the blade heavy in your pocket.

Your dad motions to the door with one arm buried in a leather jacket, while your mom shuffles out of the hallway. "What's taking you so long?" he asks. "We're late."

"Sorry. I got a lot on my mind." The three of you walk to his car. Your dad opens the passenger door for your mom.

"Does my son have a girlfriend?" Your mom turns around in her seat and smiles. "Is that your distraction?" Today she curled her hair, so now even your mom's hair looks shorter than your own. You slick yours back to make it less obvious.

If you're not going to tell them that you're gay,

you're telling them that you're straight by default. You might as well make them think you're one stud of a straight guy.

She gives your knee a hard squeeze with her manicured fingers when you shrug. "I knew you were hiding something! Who is it? I know her? I know everyone."

"No," you say quickly. "She's no one. I mean, she's great. It's nothing official."

"As long as you're having fun," she says. "But don't hurt this *chica*'s feelings."

Your dad turns off the car in the church's parking lot and looks back at you without meeting your eyes. "Don't do anything unsanctified with that girl. You hear me?"

"Yes, sir." You grab the door handle, but stop as he lays a heavy hand on your shoulder.

"I'm serious, John. Confess today."

You try to keep your tone light, but your heart is pounding. Suddenly, you feel like crying. *Pinche joto*, you fucking faggot. "We're late, remember?" You open your door and stand outside, watching your mom speak low and quickly to him, so it must be in Spanish.

Once they get out, you all walk in together—a big happy family. Your mom leans over with her arm hooked around yours and whispers, "Bring her to the dinner."

"We'll see," you say, but she just squeezes your arm tighter.

The sermon today is supposed to welcome the new family that joined the church and moved in on the other side of the freeway from Clark. They barely speak English. Father Mathus mentions a lot about acceptance and neighborliness. "When an alien resides with you in your land, you shall not oppress the alien. Leviticus 19:33." You wonder if that only counts toward aliens in origin.

Once church is over and your parents have mingled enough while the place clears out, you tell them you'll find a ride back. Your dad nods because he thinks he got through to you about confession. Your mom clings to him as he walks out the door.

You stand in front of the confessional in the back for a while, wondering at the details engraved in the wood. Even when you confess, you're hidden.

Once your parents drive away and the parking lot is empty except for Father Mathus's car, you cross yourself in front of the stained-glass window and head outside. You'll confess your own way.

You head to Tres Sonrisas down the street, making the bell ring when you pass through the door. You pick out one of the small bottles of tequila and place it on the counter in front of a tall girl in a blue vest, huge hoop earrings, and too much blue mascara over her eyes. She looks bored.

"I can't let you buy that, John," she says, shifting her eyes to the left. Maybe there's a camera over there. You're the only two people in the store.

"Do I know you?"

"Sofia . . . We go to school together. I had a crush on you in middle school." She rolls her eyes. "I was your first kiss?" She sighs, gesturing to her shirt. "Nametag, come on." Sofia Valencia.

"No, no, I remember. Sofia." You do remember. It felt like a kiss between friends or an aunt and it confused you. You ran away from her for the rest of fifth grade because you didn't want her to do it again.

You look for more money in your pocket but find nothing. "Please. I never drink."

"Clearly." She pushes the bottle toward you.

You grab it in one hand and shake it. "I'll share."

You wait patiently while she taps her foot behind the counter and chews the inside of her cheek. "Ugh, fine!" She snatches the bottle from your hand. "Let me put up the sign."

Once she puts a "Back Soon" sign up in the front window, the two of you go out the back of the store and sit. The dumpster next to you smells like piss, but you try not to think about it as you take a long swig of tequila. She takes it from your hand and drinks too.

You look at her curly brown hair and her tight clothes, her curves more obvious now that the vest's gone. You try to make yourself want her, but you don't feel anything.

"Did you go to church today?" she asks.

"Why would you ask that?"

She gestures the bottle in her hand toward your clothes.

"Oh, yeah. Church every Sunday." You motion for her to give you the bottle and she does. It takes three more gulps to make you feel warm.

"Aren't you not supposed to drink or something? 'Cause you're religious?"

Maybe it's the buzz, but you suddenly couldn't give a shit if the church or your parents would approve or not. Keeping in your secret but being treated like a fuck-up anyway is making you careless. Instead, you ask, "You're not?"

"I guess that makes me kind of badass, doesn't it?" She grins at you. You remember that about her—she always wanted to be different.

You wonder what Isaac would say about you being here as she pulls on one of her hoops and pushes your shoulder with her shoulder. She's flirting with you.

"Shut up. Man, I can't wait to get out of here," she says, looking to the left at the shops on the road.

"You'll make it out," you say, nodding, distracted by the plan forming in your head. It won't even be a lie, really. You're friends, right? And she's pretty. Not that that matters. All that matters is that she's a girl. "We all will, someday. It's just a matter of surviving until then."

"Just one more year," she says. She takes the bottle from you and raises it. "To survival."

"To survival." Sofia takes a drink before you and stands up. You feel a real buzz now. Bringing Isaac and coming out with him by your side might be the right thing to do, but all you can imagine is your dad beating the shit out of both of you and forbidding you to leave when school ends, holding back the college money.

It's only a matter of time before your secret gets out.

It's only a matter of time before the people who call you a fag at school start calling you a fag in church.

"I gotta get back to work," Sofia says. "Thanks for keeping me company, John."

"Wait," you say. You hesitate just long enough for her to notice.

She looks at you, half-smiling. "You know, I'm a very open-minded person."

To ask Sofia to the dinner, turn to page 65.

To ask Isaac to the dinner, turn to page 75.

# 4

YOU SHAKE YOUR HEAD. "I'M NOT SEEING FATHER MATHUS. YOU can't make me do that."

"Then go," he says.

You can't look at him for very long without getting the urge to hurt someone, dig your own nail into your skin. You can't stand anyone else's lies now that you've shown your own.

"So, what? You can't accept your gay son just like you can't accept the fact that you're a Mexican with a Mexican wife and a Mexican family. You taught me how to hide who I am. Not anymore. *Comprende?*" You wait for an answer. You wait for him to feel hurt or sympathetic or angry but there's no emotion at all in his eyes. He's had his mask on for so long he doesn't know how to take it off.

But you took your chance while you still could—you're not going back. You run into your room, grabbing clothes, your phone, your school books, your knife. You throw the strap over your shoulder and walk past your dad and out the door, ignoring your mom yelling at you to take the phone with Father Mathus on the other end.

You call Isaac as you wander down the street, wondering which neighbors saw you from their windows, but he doesn't pick up. Fucker tells you to come out and when you finally do, he doesn't answer his phone.

You hang up, not meeting the eye of Sarah coming out of her car or of some kids smoking cigarettes around the corner or of the old man who works at the gas station, leaning on a parking meter.

"What's up, little man?" he says. You start running, holding up your jeans with your hands, thinking of places you could go. The one place you want to go isn't picking up. You call him again, no answer.

You run alongside the freeway wall by the park. That asshole can't do this to you. Not now.

You slow down to a walk and call again, this time leaving a voicemail. "Well, I did what you wanted and it ended up exactly how I thought it would. This is why I didn't want to do this in the first place! This is your fucking fault! My family isn't like yours—you know that, don't you?" You look up toward the cemetery by the church, wondering what Father Mathus would do if he saw you right now. "No one wants a faggot," you say to Isaac. "Especially not God. Take off that stupid fucking necklace." You hang up and run out onto the street, trying not to think. You don't know why you said that. You don't know why you want to hurt him, but you do, and you can't stop now.

You don't deserve him—now he doesn't have to worry.

You spend the rest of the day wandering around downtown, trying to distract yourself, but once night time comes around, you open the gate of Oak

Hill Cemetery. You stumble to the top of the huge hill toward where the headstones become more separated, spread out among the trees. You stop by the headstone where your Grandpa Jorge was buried.

Grandpa Jorge was probably the most contradictory man you ever met, always saying one thing but meaning the other. Speaking in English about Spanish, Spanish about English. Grandpa Jorge's headstone is marked Jorge Covas Garcia. He decided, for some reason—or most likely someone decided for him—to write his epitaph in English.

*He that endureth to the end shall be saved. Matthew 10:22*

You kick at the grass. Grandpa Jorge had a beautiful wife and kids and grandkids—a family. All you'll get with Isaac is the ending of your family's perfect bloodline.

You head toward the back of the cemetery tree line between a crypt and the black iron fence behind it. You lean your head against the cement and close your eyes. You start picking at your scab until it comes loose.

You focus in on the pain. You are a person—you bleed and hurt like everyone regardless of who you are or want to be. The blood drips warm down your elbow and you wipe it off into the grass.

Even when you put on all the clothes you brought, you're still freezing the whole night, only sleeping for maybe four hours. You bum a half-eaten sandwich off a stranger and dig through today's trash where no one will see you, because what little money you have in your pocket barely gets you a soda at Taco Bell. School is in two days—then you can get real food.

But you can't sleep another night in the cemetery like you thought you could. You can't stay here like a corpse or you're going to become one.

You call Mariana, whose number she gave you from a group project a long time ago. She tells you what you want to hear before you ask.

"Hey, John! What's up? You going to my party?"

"Yeah, sure." You try to sound casual, but you can't believe how lucky you are. "I was calling to get your address."

"Absolutely," she says. When she hangs up, you realize she sounded drunk already.

---

When the sun sets, you start walking toward the suburbs past the park. You can tell it's a nicer area because of all the palm trees people don't realize are imported from Mexico, and the rows of big suburban houses with plenty of space in between for a yard, a garage. You need to be somewhere warm. You're already shivering.

You see a light in the distance, flickering behind one of the middle-class houses near West Washington. A bunch of cars are out front along the street. A sophomore from school comes out with a big can of gasoline in one hand and a bottle of vodka in the other. You grab a half-empty beer someone left on a ledge outside Mariana's house and walk past the white stucco walls and gate to the bonfire in the backyard.

They're playing the kind of music your mom

calls *cholo* music. Lots of cuss words and enough low bass that it feels like it's coming out of every wall. The bonfire lights up under people's faces and makes their eyes dark.

"Oh, hey, it's Tweedle-Dee!" A big arm hugs you around your shoulders just a little too tight to be friendly and leads you toward the fire. Lucy is dragging you forward and weighing you down at the same time. Does everyone at school know? It doesn't make sense for your parents to tell anyone about this. They would want it to fester inside, keep it hidden. That's better than having the real you as a son. "Let's go find Tweedle-Dum," Lucy says.

You look ahead. Isaac's silhouette faces the fire. You try to pull away from Lucy but he pulls you up and puts his other arm around Isaac so both of you are locked under his armpits.

"How is it going, lovebirds? Trouble in paradise?"

Isaac looks at you surprised for a minute before replying to him. "I'm doing great," he says and takes a drink. He's going to be mad at you after what he made you do?

"You guys gonna go fuck upstairs later? Because everyone wants to know exactly how that works. Who's the bitch in the relationship?"

You force yourself to speak up. "Fuck off, Lucy. We're just trying to have a good time like everybody else." Isaac looks at you, surprised that you cussed him out. You're always quiet. It feels good to drop the pretenses. You try again to pull yourself out of his grasp but he keeps you locked in. You just have to wait.

"So you're not gay?" Lucy asks. You can smell the alcohol on his breath.

You and Isaac look at each other. "No," you say. You're angry all over again, seeing Isaac shaking his head like he's disappointed in you, when he doesn't know shit about what it really means to come out—you're facing homelessness and starvation and he wants to judge you for wishing you could have avoided it.

He had to be the one to tell them about you. No one else knows. No one else would want to.

"No?" He spins you in front of him. You stumble back. You recognize a few people now, slowly making their way over to surround you and the fire. They're all ready for a fight, nudging each other for a better view. One girl climbs on some guy's shoulders to see better.

Lucy keeps Isaac locked in and rubs his knuckles on his skull, hard. "Come on. Tell me the truth. Is John a fag like you?"

You're about to shove him away from Isaac before it gets worse, which you know it will. He's just a punching bag. A toy. You will be too if he tells him the truth.

"Wait!" Mariana comes out of the crowd, her long black hair swinging. "I know how John can prove it."

People laugh and yell a low, "Ooh." You swallow hard.

Lucy puts one fist over his mouth, keeping his other arm hooked around Isaac's neck. "Okay, okay. John, you gonna fuck this slut?"

She laces her fingers between yours. Everyone's eyes are locked onto you.

"You not gonna stop me, Lucy?" she says, clearly drunk. Lucy just grins and Mariana practically breathes out beer. "Let's see how you like to see your girlfriend with someone else, asshole." A few more people join the circle around the four of you, some pulling out phones to take a video, a few yelling at Lucy to just hit him already. It's the ultimate showdown. Drama, gossip, violence, sex—all at once. You're nothing but a spectacle.

"Go ahead," Lucy says, sounding totally unconcerned, distracted by Isaac, who pulls out of his headlock. It's apparently exactly what Lucy wanted, because he lets him go completely, almost sending him falling into the fire. He blows hair out of his eyes and looks at Lucy, waiting for whatever's next.

The crowd starts yelling all at once, so you can't hear what any of them are saying. Mariana looks at you, still holding your hand.

"Well?" she says, speaking loud enough that everyone inside and outside the house can hear her. "Gonna fuck me? Or are you too queer?"

To let her take you inside, turn to page 88.
To help Isaac up, turn to page 104.

# 5

SAINT MARY'S CHURCH IS TOO CLOSE TO YOUR HOUSE—THERE'S NEVER an excuse not to go on Sunday or confess almost at the same moment you sin. The cross on the roof looks out over Clark Street by the gas station as if it were any other local business selling prayer candles. The little box of a place was once some kind of ancient, official building for the city—now it's just a flat room with votive candles, pews, replaced stained-glass windows, and Father Mathus.

You zip up your jacket even though it's probably seventy outside and step toward the double doors.

Father Mathus, a thin man with salt-and-pepper hair, motions you inside, expecting you since your parents called to say you'd be in as soon as possible. Your dad's Toyota pulls out of the parking lot as the doors close. They wanted you to come alone in case someone sees them dragging their kid to church during off-hours.

"Your mom asked me to make sure we have a few visits through the rest of the school year. I'm excited to get to know you, Mr. Garcia." His voice sounds different when he's not speaking to everyone at the congregation or your parents afterwards. He's louder, more intense.

"You baptized me," you say, following his black robe down the aisle. "You already know me."

"Whoever believes and is baptized will be saved. Whoever believes." He looks at you as he opens the door to his office. "Do you still have your faith?"

You walk past him into his office, keeping your voice steady. You want to ask, "Should I?" but you're here to be who you should be. "Of course. I wouldn't be here if I didn't." He looks skeptical so you change the subject. "How many Hail Marys?"

"Let's save that for the end of our session," he says, sitting in his chair on the other side of the desk. The door is open. You hear footsteps and someone whispering to herself by the pulpit. You could still run—it can't be that bad out there alone.

"Please sit," he says. Immediately, you do. He holds your salvation in his hands. You examine the cross behind him—a detailed stained-glass window that you've only seen from the parking lot outside. All it's hiding is a shitty office desk and chair, papers and mail lined up neatly in stacks everywhere, an open filing cabinet. "What is Isaac doing today?"

Your stomach catches in your throat. "What kind of question is that?"

"This town knows about his predisposition to sin, although that's not the problem. His mistake is in not acknowledging the sin and therefore not working toward salvation." He leans forward confidentially. "You, on the other hand, still have a chance. What is your relationship with Isaac?"

You hold your breath and look down.

"If you don't answer the question, I'll have to report it back to your mother after our session. What are your feelings about Isaac?"

You look at him for a long time. He's stern, with unwavering brown eyes, but there's also genuine concern. He believes what he's saying. He wants to save you. "I don't know."

"Do you speak to each other at school?"

"Not really."

"Not really? He's your friend."

You fight the urge to stand up and look down on him. "I didn't say that."

"So, he's not your friend."

"I mean," you stutter, not knowing how much he knows. You wonder what he's doing now. You wonder if anyone else has found out about you since you told your parents. You thought you could handle coming here once a week and talking about scriptures, doing reparations, lying your way back home. But if he makes you talk about Isaac, you won't be able to hide it. "We talk sometimes."

He leans back, locking his fingers together and you look away. "That's what I was looking for, John. Honesty. But that's not the whole truth is it?"

"Is this a fucking interrogation?"

"Watch your language." You close your mouth. What's gotten into you? You can't keep your two selves in check. They're overlapping. Talking about Isaac in church makes you feel like you're lying and telling the truth at the same time.

"I think I've had enough counseling today," you say, standing up.

He keeps his gaze steady, like each question is exactly the same. "Are you having a sexual relationship with Isaac?"

You feel yourself flinch back before answering, "Priests believe in high school rumors now?" You wonder if Isaac ever confessed to him, but shake it off. He never used to think being gay was something to confess about and he's as religious as anyone.

"I'll tell your parents you're not answering my questions, John. I'm only trying to assist you in saving yourself." He stands up to look at the cross window. "I've known the Garcia family for a long time."

"What are you saying? I'm ruining my family?"

"Do you believe you are a homosexual, John?"

When he turns toward you, you don't look away from his eyes.

"Answer the question."

"You know the answer to that. Don't make me say it."

"Confess."

"This is different. It's not—"

"A sin? It's one sin among many. Answer the question or I will give a report to your parents. If you answer now, I'll tell them you're improving. Have you had a sexual relationship with Isaac Hernandez?"

You grit your teeth, still unable to leave or turn away. Nothing is stopping you from running except for the light coming through the stained glass, the silence on the other side of the walls, and Father Mathus's voice.

The truth is you want to get better. You always have.

Carefully, you nod.

"Do you believe you are a homosexual?"

It's too much. You have to keep your face from changing, keep your gaze on his face steady, even as you're crying. Something softens in Father Mathus and he stands up, moving toward the door. "I'm sorry to upset you. That will be all for today."

You turn as quickly as you can down the aisle, past your neighbor, Sarah, who's sitting in one of the pews. You pull your hood over your face to cover your eyes.

"Hey, John. You okay?"

You jog down Clark toward the cemetery opposite the park. You stay as late as you can and ignore everyone's calls—including Isaac's, maybe he heard what happened, maybe not—before going home when you think your parents will be asleep, but when you get there your dad is watching TV.

"How did it go?" he asks, raising his beer.

"Exactly how you wanted it to go." You can't be alone fast enough and close your bedroom door behind you too loud, making the prayer candles on your floor rattle against the wall. You grab your knife from the bedside table and pull up your pant leg once you're sure your dad isn't going to come in and yell at you about slamming doors.

You press the blade into your calf instead of slicing it. You hold it there for a while, trying to keep your breathing steady and not make any noise. When you finally pull it out, you have to hold all the blood in with the palm of your hand and wash it off with a water bottle and a towel. You hold it against your leg, lean back on your headboard, and close your eyes, falling deeper into the sting, thinking about nothing.

You have one session every week. Every week, Father Mathus gets you to say more about Isaac and how you feel about him, quoting verses at you, and, by the third week, finally starts giving you steps toward repentance. He watches you do the

Hail Marys and light the candles. He watches you fall deeper into some kind of nameless, unfeeling place where the things that happen around you can't touch you. You go through the motions every day until you can be yourself again in your room at night, cutting along your bone until every memory of that day replaces itself with just blank, white-hot pain. The Hail Marys aren't enough to pay for your sins.

But you still don't understand how you're supposed to be good when you were born the wrong way. How can you be good when you have to lie to do it?

The first step is that you can't talk to Isaac anymore—that's part of the deal Father Mathus made to you, but that's something you had already promised yourself anyway. He's the one who is making you sick. He's putting thoughts in your head because he's lonely, ostracized by what he's done to himself. He just wanted you to sin with him to make him feel right.

One day you walk into your room after a session, itching to feel that steel slip under your skin, and Isaac is standing by your bed. He looks more worn than you've ever seen him. His hair has grown out. You can tell he's having a bad night, because his arms are crossed and he's trying to act tough again. You've seen what the guys at school have done to him. Not having you there to talk about it with must be killing him. He can't self-console like you can.

But those are thoughts from before.

"What are you doing to yourself, John?" He's whispering so you know he came in through the window. Your mom is in the living room, going over bills.

"I'm not allowed to talk to you." You look at the knife on your bed. "Just get out of here before someone sees you. Please."

"I heard what happened. I guess it's working, too. They taught you how to kill the part of you that loves."

"Leviticus 20:13."

"I don't give a shit about whatever some bigoted asshole wrote a thousand years ago." Hearing anger again, honesty again, briefly makes you feel better, but it goes away. "The religion I believe in accepts people like us. You know why? Because we're good people. At least I thought you were."

"We're not good," you say, opening the window. "The sooner you accept that the better. Go, Isaac. This is trespassing."

"I know you. You don't even believe what you're saying."

"I know what the Bible says."

"You know what the Bible means," he says, throwing his hands up. You wonder if the neighbors can hear him. You dad would freak out if he knew Isaac was here. "And you know who you are. You know this can't change you, even if you tried."

"I'm not a faggot like you." You keep your expression strong.

Isaac looks away from you quickly before

climbing out the window. You only notice how tired and red his eyes are, maybe from crying, when he steps into the light outside your apartment. He's really been having a hard time without you.

He backs away, but before you close the window you ask, "What does the Bible mean, anyway?"

He rolls his eyes and you notice his cross necklace outside of his shirt. "That's your problem, Jay. You can't keep letting other people decide your beliefs for you."

You pull the black curtains over quickly, refusing to look at him as you do, and lay down on the bed, flipping open the pocket knife after a few minutes of trying to ignore it. You dig the point between the veins in your left wrist and aim down. Then you turn it, twisting it under the skin and the sharpness of the pain that comes is so intense you have to put your other wrist in your mouth and bite down. You dig deeper because you still love Isaac and you still want to be with him and the pain suddenly isn't helping you ignore this anymore, it all just hurts.

The blood pools around your blanket. You're too tired to fight it. You get dizzy at the same moment your mom walks in and the room goes dark.

————————————————

You wake up to the smell of flowers. When you open your eyes, a bouquet is on the table by your hospital bed from Mr. Alfaro. You'd sit up, but pushing down with your left hand hurts.

Under the flowers is a pamphlet.

TRUTH SPORTS CAMP

FIND YOUR TRUE SELF UNDER THE LIGHT OF GOD

JUNE 2 – JUNE 23

It's not over. Will it ever be? You cover your eyes with your hands. Whatever's fucked up with their son's head can be fixed by force. You spend the next three days on lockdown in the hospital for a psych evaluation. When the doctors bring in your parents, your mom cries through the whole meeting, yelling out again and again that nothing is helping you. Your dad just shakes his head because it's not manly to cry. You realize that this pamphlet is their last attempt to fix the unfixable. The new solution is a gay camp. But like Isaac said, you can't change. If you try, you'll end up killing yourself.

You didn't meet God during your near-death experience or see heaven or hell. There was only peaceful silence. You wonder if maybe that's enough.

To use the camp as an excuse to run, turn to page 114.

To refuse to go to the camp, turn to page 153.

**A**FTER LEAVING SOFIA AT HER WORK, YOU CALL ISAAC TO TELL HIM you're going to your aunt's house for your birthday alone. He's upset, saying you could bring him as a friend. You try to lighten the mood because if you don't, you might break down.

"Your big mouth is going to get us in trouble again." But he doesn't joke back this time. He tells you goodnight.

Before you go to sleep you dig the blade into your right thigh, since you ran out of room on your shoulders. You think about how happy she was that you asked her to go to the party with you. You remember moving close to her and kissing her, touching her body. She told you to slow down. The anguish inside you makes you press the blade in further. The spot feels new—a pain that makes your toes curl. You press it harder until it feels like you're going to pass out.

You barely sleep and everything feels off in the morning—how your clothes fit, how long your hair has gotten, your scars. Everything goes by in a blur. Your mom makes you *chilaquiles* with fried eggs. Your dad gets your present out of the back room. A nice button-up, gray shirt—the kind you can only really wear to church. You say thank you. When he goes to the bathroom, you say *gracias* to your mom.

You put the shirt on for the dinner, and the sleeves are long enough to cover most of the scars. The end of a longer one is visible around the collar, but not enough to draw attention. When you come out of your room, you say she's meeting you there. Your parents ask who, and you say, "Sofia. Just a girl." When your dad looks at you skeptically and your mom gives you a hug, you say, *"Novia."* Then add, "Girlfriend."

Your aunt's house is huge and pristine com-
pared to your tiny, shitty apartment. You hug your
family members one by one: your Aunt Lisa, your
Grandma Cleo and her husband John, who you
were named after but never talk to, the five cousins
from your aunt's various past lovers and husbands,
and your *abuelita*. The rest of the family is stuck in
Mexico.

When the doorbell rings a few minutes later,
your attention goes straight to your dad, who looks
at you sternly. "Well? Let her in."

Sofia is dressed in a tight black dress, which
you think is inappropriate for a birthday, but she
looks presentable enough. You look back and forth
between her and your dad, who shakes her hand,
and your mom, who hugs her for too long. Your
cousins crowd around her in the foyer, cooing about
her long, pretty hair.

"It's nice to meet you all," she says. She's chewing
gum for some reason and has to spit it out in the
trash before sitting down for dinner.

"John, would you like to say grace?" your aunt asks from across the huge table. Everyone sits around it quietly, even the kids. Sofia sits next to you.

"English or Spanish?" you ask her, but look at your dad.

"Oh—" your aunt starts, but he interrupts her.

"English will be fine. We don't want to confuse your friend, here." He looks down at Sofia across the table.

"Oh, I speak—" You grab her knee before she can finish. Your dad will like her better the whiter she seems. She looks at you and starts coughing to cover it up.

"I'll just start," you say. "Bless us, O Lord, and these, thy gifts, which we—" You look up, suddenly feeling sick. Everyone's eyes are closed, hands are clasped, heads down. Sofia looks at you and gives you an encouraging smile, then pries her hand from yours and drops it to your knee, then slides it up to your thigh. You clear your throat. "Which we are about to—"

She squeezes your thigh and you stand up, knocking into your cousin, who looks up and shouts, "Hey!"

"I feel sick—I'm sorry—"

You walk quickly down the hallway, hearing everyone mutter and your aunt's shrill voice asking you if you need help. You run the tap in the bathroom trying to cover up the sound of you practically hyperventilating. Tonight is supposed to feel right and all you've done is pussy out.

You start crying, because you can't even pretend.

You need to cut yourself. Maybe if you do one real quick, you can get through the rest of the night. You start throwing open the drawers in their bathroom, frantically looking for something sharp enough to pierce through skin. Guess they don't need that here. There's nothing but toothbrushes and lotions.

"Juan?" It's your mom. You wipe your face quickly, trying to breathe.

"What?" You overcompensate and your voice sounds harsh.

"Your friend Isaac is here. He said he couldn't believe you forgot to tell us about him."

You look away from the mirror. This isn't happening. You have to close your eyes for a minute before you open the door and follow her back into the dining room. He's there all right, sitting at the table with a plate of food in front of him. They'd pushed in another chair just for him. The small part of you that isn't completely horrified knows that you've always wanted to see him sitting with your family, like they have accepted him, which would mean that they had accepted you.

His face is flushed and he looks up at you with half-open eyes. "Hey, buddy! Welcome to the party. Hey, happy birthday."

He's drunk, sloshed actually, and any guilt you might have locked away for not inviting him immediately turns into rage. You manage to clear your throat enough to speak clearly. "What are you doing here?"

He stands up and pats one of your cousins on the

head before walking over to you. "You invited me," he says, and nods like he's trying to reassure himself that it's true. He looks like he's tearing up.

"Oh," you say. Not here, Isaac. Please. "I must have forgotten." You see your dad stand up and cross his arms, giving you a look that says you'll hear from him later.

Isaac then pulls you in for a hug and you don't hug back. He holds you tighter. "Hug me back," he says through his teeth. He even shakes you a little, but you don't move. You've never been more terrified. Should you tell them now?

"Alright, what the hell is going on?" Sofia says. Now she's standing up.

Isaac holds your shoulders and looks into your eyes with his bloodshot ones. "Did you bring her?"

But you can't. You just can't. "Isaac, you should go." You try to grab his shoulder so you can push him toward the door, but he turns to your family.

"She's not real." He gestures to Sofia, leaning so far forward that he almost falls. "She's just a decoy for your gay son. That's just how scared he is of all of you fucking dickheads who won't accept anyone who's different from you." Isaac is shouting and crying now. He looks at Sofia. "He's with me."

As he talks, everyone around the table stands up, even the little cousins and your elderly grandma. Most of the women have hands over their mouths and look tentatively between you and Isaac. Your grandpa is sitting down with his hand over his forehead. Your dad walks closer, grabs a handful of Isaac's shirt and twists his body around. He starts pushing against his back like he's herding cattle.

"What the fuck, Jay!" Isaac looks back at you but it's like you're behind a glass wall. You're mortified, a statue. Every time you've daydreamed about coming out to your family, it's never ended as bad as this. "Man up and stop him!"

"I'm not gay," you say to him, then to everyone. "I'm not gay. He's just obsessed with me. He's just—he's crazy, he's a liar."

Your mom puts her arm around your shoulders

and pulls you away from Isaac as your dad pushes him out the door. Isaac shouts, "We're over, asshole!" before the door slams in his face.

Everything is quiet for a moment before your dad glares at you.

"I told you," you say, taking a step back. "He's crazy. I'm with Sofia." You walk over to her and put your arm around her waist. It feels awkward, unnatural, like a puppeteer is moving your body instead of you, but Sofia shoves you away.

"You piece of shit," she says. "I can't believe you were gay this whole time, you piece of shit!"

"I'm not a fucking faggot."

Sofia grabs her jacket and walks back through the house. One of your little cousins is staring at you. These people were supposed to protect you no matter what and now they don't even see a person anymore—not even Isaac sees you. These people were supposed to love you, even if they can't forgive you.

You can't help it. You turn and almost run back

through the house. Your mom shouts, "Juan. *Por favor.*"

You're out the door, but your dad's voice reaches you anyway. "John! Get back here!"

"You think you're not going to hell for this?" The voice belongs to your aunt. You scratch your arm hard with your fingernails as your *abuelita* tells her to be quiet. You slam the front door closed.

You don't belong there. You don't care. Fuck this life. Fuck all of them if they won't see you for you.

You keep walking in the dark and the cold until you reach a stop sign where the roads stretch out far in either direction. You can either go right toward your high school or left toward the church. Both will give you a place to sleep for the night.

To go to the church, turn to page 123.

To go to the high school, turn to page 130.

# 7

YOU LOOK UP AT HER. "YOU HAVE TO GET BACK TO WORK."
She looks disappointed. She had a crush on you before. Maybe she still has one now. You swallow back the taste of tequila still in your mouth. "Thanks, though."

"For what?" she asks.

You raise the bottle. "Thanks for hanging out with me." You don't mention the fact that you're surprised she hasn't heard the rumors.

"You know where to find me."

Once the heavy door clicks closed you take a long drink and look back at your phone. It feels like you're going to throw up. You don't want to do this.

Then again, even if he did spread the rumors to make you come out, Isaac's the only one who's always been there when you need him. Isaac is all that matters and the only way to truly be with Isaac is to tell the truth. That's what he's been saying all along.

That night you don't cut yourself like usual. Instead, you clean off the blade with your mom's nail polish remover, digging in the cracks of your initials engraved on the handle, praying it's the last time you'll ever need to touch it. It has to be the last.

The next morning you put on the shirt your parents got you for your birthday and you have your special birthday breakfast, *chilaquiles* and eggs. A few times you try to open your mouth to tell them that you invited Isaac to the dinner, remembering how excited he was when you called him, but your jaw clamps shut and you grind your teeth. They know who he is, *what* he is.

"Okay there, John?" your dad asks, dropping his fork to his plate.

"Absolutely." You try to hide behind a smile, but your dad looks you up and down quickly and raises his eyebrow. Thankfully, he continues eating, but you know that he thinks you're acting weird.

Once you get back to your room you start pacing, running your hand through your hair, rolling the sleeves of your new shirt up and down, fidgeting with your knife. You jump when Isaac knocks on your window.

"Let me in, fucker. Someone's coming."

"Shit." You jog over so you can pull back the screen. "Well, we won't need to sneak around after today."

He climbs inside while you put the screen back and close the curtains. When you look back at him, he's staring at the cross on your wall.

You check your bedroom door to see if it's locked and then walk up to him. He holds you automatically when you put your arms around him.

"Sorry," he says. "I'm nervous."

"This was your idea."

He puts his hand over his eyes and pulls down.

"I'll be fine. I just don't want to fuck with everything you have going here."

"What? I don't see anything here worth saving the lie for." You barely believe it and he can tell. You have your whole life to lose, but you're going to be strong. Do it for Isaac if you can't manage to do it for yourself. "Let's just talk about something else."

He tries to smile at you, but you can tell he's forcing it. "Hey, happy birthday. New shirt? Very sexy—"

You freeze at a knock on the door. "Hide," you whisper. He walks quietly around you and pulls the closet door closed with him on the other side.

You take a deep breath and open the bedroom door. "Sorry, I was changing."

"I thought I heard voices," your dad says, looking past you into the room.

"I was talking to myself." You step aside as he walks in, but it's too late to stop him from seeing it.

"Is that a new jacket?" he asks. He ticks his chin to Isaac's black hoodie on the floor where he dropped it. Your mouth feels dry.

"Yeah. It's mine," you say.

"You can't afford that, John, where'd it come from?"

"I found it," you say. "Someone just left it at school."

"John." He gets closer to you, making him seem even taller. "Stealing is a sin. It's your birthday so I'm going to let it slide, but you need to return that jacket to the lost and found at school, got it? First thing tomorrow."

You let out a long breath. "Yeah. I will."

"Got it?" he says again, louder.

"Yes, sir."

He looks around your room. "You bringing your girlfriend to dinner?"

Your heart is pounding. "No, a friend."

He looks over the room one last time before closing the door behind him.

"Holy shit," you whisper. You turn to Isaac as he steps out. "You actually came out of the closet."

He looks more nervous than you've ever seen

him. "Can we not joke about this right now? Your dad almost killed you over a jacket."

"You know how he is." You try to act casual. "Don't worry."

"I don't know," he says. "I don't want you to get hurt."

"Come on, Isaac, why are you doing this? You always knew the consequences. You convinced me anyway—"

"The second I step in there, all the rumors about you are going to be legitimate. School has never been this bad and I don't know why. I don't know. I have a bad feeling."

Why is he nervous if he's been spreading the rumors about you? You breathe out, relieved. Maybe he didn't tell everyone, after all. "Is that really the reason?" He shrugs, which makes you nervous. "I'll be fine. Just like you've been telling me for years— this is gonna fix everything."

All he can do is nod. He says he needs to get ready and swings himself back out your window.

Your aunt's house is a big, two-story suburban east of the park. You hug your overly shrill aunt, your scrambling cousins, and quiet grandparents and greet their happy birthdays with a half-hearted smile. You can barely take in all of the noise and commotion because you're trying to figure out the best way to say it.

"This is my boyfriend, Isaac."

"I'm gay. This is Isaac. He's my boyfriend and has been for a long time. We're in love and there's nothing you can do to stop that."

"Everyone, I have something to say."

The doorbell rings a half hour later as the food is set up. "It's him," you say, feeling your voice shake but you can't stop it. "I'll get it."

Your *abuelita*, one of your favorite family members by far, says, "Oh, good!"

"Him? I thought you were bringing your girl-friend," your aunt says. Everyone is helping set the plates on the table. You put down the napkins you're handing out and walk to the foyer to open the door.

He looks nice. A pink button-up shirt and his hair slicked back. You try to give him a reassuring smile, but he looks like he's going to be sick.

You grab his arm to pull him over to the dining room, but he pushes your hand off when you turn the corner. You try to reassure him, but you can't even make yourself smile. It feels like this moment has been speeding toward you for your entire life. "This is Isaac," you finally say. Your *abuelita* looks up from her handful of forks and walks over to you.

Your dad stands up. "Hernandez?" Isaac nods, not able to smile like his usual self. He looks like a different person without his confidence. Everyone is looking at him like he's a homeless person off the street trying to make a place at the table, instead of your friend.

"You speak Spanish? *Como estas?*" your *abuelita* asks.

"*Hola, señora,*" he says. He holds out a hand to her, but she pulls him in for a hug—she's the only one treating him like a real person. You feel so relieved you just want to shout it.

"I have something to say," you start. You're barely nervous anymore. "It's important."

She pulls back and Isaac looks at you. He grabs your arm and squeezes. "No," he says quickly. He pulls both of you backwards. "I changed my mind. Please."

You look between his wide-eyed look and your family's steady gaze. "Well, get on with it," your *abuelita* says. "You're holding up the dinner I made."

"Hush," your Dad's mom, grandma Cleo says, giving you a glare so harsh you can't meet it.

Isaac clears his throat at the same time you start to speak. You still want to say it, but Isaac beats you to it.

"John just wanted to say that we're both trying to go to college after high school."

There are some sighs and congratulatory remarks, but your ears are ringing. "Excuse me." You walk away and out the door. The nighttime air chills you from head to toe.

When Isaac finally follows you out, you turn to him and try to keep your voice low. "What the fuck, Isaac? I thought we had a plan."

"I couldn't. I can't, I'm sorry." He tries to grab your hand but stops himself. "You saw how they looked at me," he says, keeping his voice quiet. "I wanted you to do it before when shit wasn't so bad, but now—everyone at school—"

"So?"

"So, I have a home to go back to after a shit day. You can't handle it, Jay. I just know you. If you don't have your family, I don't know what you'll do." He looks down the street at the headlights of a passing truck.

"I get sad sometimes," you say. "That's it." He doesn't answer and won't look at you. "That's what people do when they know they're doing the wrong thing."

"Being with me is wrong, now?" He shakes his

head, looking up at the sky. "Fine. I'm glad you've been pushed around at school like I have, but I'm not letting it get any worse. This is the last thing I'm doing for you. Asshole." He starts walking down the driveway to the street. When he's a few yards away, he wipes his eyes with his sleeve.

You fumble for your knife in your pocket. He can't leave. "You're the one making it worse." You hold the blade against your wrist—a place you usually try to avoid and slice down over the bone when he barely gives you a second glance.

He looks away, nothing in his expression. You're shaking hard and you want to squeeze your arm to stop the pain, but you hold back. "You think you can handle coming out to your parents?" he says, looking at you and trying hard to avoid seeing your arm. "I didn't cut you. You did. I can't be responsible for you anymore."

You take a few steps forward, trying to ignore the burn in your wrist. You watch him pull out onto the road in his car before you go back inside, not caring who sees the blood run down your hand onto the floor.

Your whole family practically screams when you come in. Everyone starts petting you and asking what happened. You don't say anything back. Your shoulders are shaking and you put your head in your hands.

"I'll take care of it." It's your dad's voice. When you look up, he reaches for your arm and pushes you back toward the door. "Sorry, everybody. We'll have to postpone the dinner."

He shoves you into the back of his car and he and your mom get in the front.

"You're getting help," your dad says. Your mom is staring at the floor. "I don't know what the hell you were thinking, bringing that kid, but he's obviously a bad influence. He carries sin with him wherever he goes. You need to stay away from him."

All you can do is shake your head and look out the window at the road falling behind you. That won't be a problem anymore.

"You hear me? You're getting help," he says. He

makes a sharp turn, throwing you against the seat. "*Me entiendes?*"

You pull the towel on your wrist back over the wound, sending a whole new stinging sensation up your arm, all the way to the elbow. You lean back and close your eyes, letting the car push your nails against the skin.

To refuse his help and fix things with Isaac, turn to page 153.

To accept his help and leave Isaac alone, turn to page 164.

YOU PUSH YOUR GUILT ASIDE TO DEAL WITH WHEN YOU'RE ALONE. YOU kiss Mariana hard on the mouth, pretending that it's Isaac's lips and his hair in your hand by his neck.

You release her and she smirks. The crowd opens up to see Lucy's reaction, but you ignore him. You step toward Isaac who won't look at you. You put your hand out to help him up, but he doesn't take it.

"Come on, Isaac."

"Go ahead," Lucy says. "Help your boyfriend."

Isaac won't reach for it. You don't know if he's mad about you kissing Mariana or about your voice-mail or both.

Before you can try to convince him, Lucy says to

the crowd, "There you have it. Queer as shit." You pull your hand back, trying to not want to hit Isaac yourself.

This is your second chance. Maybe Isaac wants you to do this because he knows if you tell them the truth, you'll be the one on the ground. You flip around before he can see how close you are to crying, because you know he'll see right through you. You grab Mariana's hand and pull her toward the house.

"You're hurting me," she says, but no one can hear over the yelling. A group follows you inside, talking loudly, urging you on. You're relieved when you see Isaac in the back behind Lucy, hands in his pockets—safe. He doesn't look mad or upset, just blank. You breathe out and walk faster. Being a good person—surviving—is about making sacrifices.

"Where?"

She glares at you briefly before pointing to a door on the left. You pull her inside, close it, lock it. You can hear muffled talking outside and a bang on the door.

The room is dark and you can only see the shapes of her bed behind her, a dresser to the left, a window. She doesn't move and neither do you until the sounds outside the bedroom quiet down.

She's still holding your hand, even though you're alone. "I think we can hide in here until they settle down," you say.

"So you really are gay?" She pushes herself against you.

You shake your head, close to tears again. "Please. I'm trying to be a good person. I don't want to do this to you."

"I'll help you," she says, using a different voice than she used outside. She's trying to sound sexy now, but she still just sounds drunk.

You whisper as quietly as you can. "Look. I don't—I don't know. I'm not a bad person," you say. You don't know why you keep saying it to her.

"You're not a bad person, John," she says. She kisses your neck and your whole body tenses up. This is wrong. "You're not a bad person."

She says it one more time before you let her touch you and you touch her back, but it's awkward and your hands are shaky. When you finally leave the room as she's fixing her makeup in the mirror, the group outside has dispersed, and you're not sure why you did what you did. No one even cares.

You scan the faces of the crowd in the living room, but Isaac's not there. The party is dying down, with only a few people left sitting around, smoking, or talking. Not even Lucy had the patience to stick around and find out if you could fuck his girlfriend.

You grab your right wrist with your left hand and squeeze it as hard as you can. You open doors along the hallway, looking for Isaac. One door opens up to a bathroom where you see people passing around a red cup. You sit down and grab it from someone's hands, taking a long drink.

Some girl says, "Whoa, slow down, man. That stuff's, like, illegal."

You remember getting into the bathtub at some point. You remember telling everyone to be quiet, because you need to sleep.

You wake up early the next morning, head

throbbing. You get out and call home before Mariana can see you stayed there all night. Once you reach the park, you sit in one of the swings and dial your mom's work instead. You ask for Susana.

"What is it? Juan, are you okay?" You wonder who's watching her now, making sure she speaks English.

"I have to come home, Mom. Please. I have school tomorrow."

"Your father—"

"I don't care what I have to do. I just want to go home." Your voice is rising too high. You try to breathe normally.

"Okay, okay," she says. There's a silence. "Listen, come after school tomorrow. I have to prepare your father."

"Please, let me stay tonight."

"One more night," she says. "That's all we ask. One more night to think about what you have done."

You stand up off the swing and don't say anything, heading toward the church.

"*Te amo*," you say.

You look down, eyes closed at her hesitation before she says, "*Te amo*. See you tomorrow." You hang up, shivering, as you reach the church, trying to make yourself go inside, but you can't. The walls will see right through you. You spend the rest of the day walking up and down Clark Street. You stay at the cemetery again, only able to sleep once you distract yourself enough with the pain you dig into your shoulder. Something is different this time. It doesn't work. You keep saying his name, *Isaac*.

---

At school the next day, your only goal is to see him. You move like a ghost through your classes, and only hear one or two comments about what happened the night before—everyone still is in shock that Lucy didn't kill you for sleeping with Mariana. You walk away when a couple of people make jokes about Isaac.

Isaac finds you sitting behind the cafeteria wall during lunch. He's in his usual black hoodie with his hands in the pockets of his jeans. He stands over you.

"Why did you do that?"

You put your backpack down and stand to face him. You're mostly hidden here—a fence behind you with trees behind that, the cafeteria on the other side. People will only see you if they come from between the buildings. "I was protecting you. Lucy was going to kill you."

He breathes out and finally meets your eyes. You recognize the puppy-dog look on his face and prepare for him to say something you don't like. "Do you love me?"

It takes you a while, but finally you nod. Why does every part of you feel numb? Why can't you figure out who you are anymore? He steps closer, looking nervous, which is odd for him as he is the one who is always happy, always joking. *No pienses en el.* He kisses you until you lift your hands up and hold his face. You both push hard against each other.

You're together again. You could almost cry,

because you feel that release again, and it's better than when the blade sinks beneath your skin. You're who you really are, with the person you really love.

"Holy shit!" You pull away from him and see one of Lucy's friends with his phone out, smiling at you. "Holy fucking shit!"

A few other people sitting outside come over from the cafeteria courtyard. "Did you know he was there?" you say, suddenly understanding. "What the hell did you do?"

Mariana and her friends whisper behind you and one of them laughs. Mariana doesn't look embarrassed, just triumphant.

Isaac stares into your eyes, not even hesitating when he sees you breathing unsteadily. "You fucked me over last night. Now you don't get a choice."

"You're a fucking psychopath," you say, sounding nasal from crying. You grab your backpack.

"Hey, come on. Kiss again!" the same guy says, holding his phone up. Mariana's friends shout in agreement. Other people start joining the circle. "Don't be sad."

You walk around the corner to see everyone staring from their separate groups. They could all see you. This was Isaac's plan.

"You fucked Mariana, you asshole!" Isaac yells. You start running down the steps and away from the school.

When you finally reach your apartment, you're out of breath. You try your key and have to yank it out with both hands when it gets jammed. You find somewhere beyond the gate to the main office and wait, keeping an eye on your door. Mr. Alfaro waves to you from the office and you do what you've always wanted to do. You flip him off. He says a couple of things in Spanish under his breath, but you can't catch it before he goes inside, watching you the whole way.

Finally you hear a car on the road. A few minutes later your mom turns the corner, jostling with her groceries and looking tired as usual. You follow her inside, closing the door behind you.

"*Hijo*," she says, worried, speaking quietly in case someone hears.

"Mom. Please. I need help."

"You're early." Reluctantly, your mom hugs you back. You can't seem to let go. You close your eyes when you see the family altar over her shoulder.

"I didn't get your room finished."

"Finished?" You pull away and walk toward your bedroom door. The few things you have inside are packed up in boxes, your sheets are folded, and your mattress is bare. Only the crucifix is still up on the wall.

"Why the hell did you do that?"

"You moved out," she says. You grab the boxes of your clothes and random old toys and dump them on the floor. You put things back in your drawers, not caring whether or not that's where they went before.

Your mom stands in the doorway with her hands held together, looking small. "We make a nice office for your father. A desk by the window." She points, but you grab the door and push her out.

"This is my room. This is my stuff." You push the

door with your shoulder, but she pushes back. You really have to shove it to close it and you hear her shriek.

"Juan!" she says, then, "Thank God." There's movement on the other side of the door—footsteps. You set your alarm back on the side of your bed. You pull your sheets over the mattress, listening to whispers outside the door but it's like your ears are ringing and you can't tell who it is. There are three boxes in the corner holding everything you own and most of it is clothes and candles. They didn't even want the fucking candles anymore. They're tainted now. They were going to get rid of everything you had touched. Just like how they'd gotten rid of you.

You jump when you hear a man's voice—your dad's voice—quickly before it fades again. You shiver, suddenly terrified of him the way you were when you were a kid. Terrified and admiring. Same thing. But it's too late for him to see that side of you. He let you go. You're nothing to him. You think you hear three voices, but you're not sure. Maybe you're going crazy.

You finally get the end of the sheet over the fourth corner of the mattress and step back, wiping your eyes. This is good. This is progress—reverse progress. You're getting back to where you started. A bang on the door makes you flinch down at your shoes. It's a familiar sound—your dad when you haven't done the chores, but louder. You glance at the box of candles. You don't know if you should take them out. You don't know if that's okay.

"John, you get out here right now," your dad says. "I brought someone to talk to you."

You rub your eyes with both palms, like you could blot out the world if you press down hard enough, blind you from everything and become invisible at the same time.

"Father Mathus is here," he says.

"Son?" Father Mathus's voice makes you step back against the bed, like the voice is some creature that can break through the door any second and slit your throat. It's the voice of your conscience, speaking in your ear every day since you were born. You didn't hear him come in. He had no footsteps, just a disembodied voice. "I'm here to help."

You collapse on the bed, unfolding another sheet while you stare at the ceiling, unblinking. Father Mathus's brash voice pushes at the door again, almost physical, like two monstrous hands. "Listen to me, John. We can talk through this and get everything back to normal. You have to confess that what you've done is a sin."

You shake your head and pull your knife out of your backpack. You cut yourself quickly and cleanly on your thigh, biting on the sheet so you don't say anything. It doesn't work. You're still thinking, still running through the different ways to handle this: lie, be honest, stand up straight, be yourself, be who you want to be. You cut yourself again, but you're still thinking about Isaac, kissing you like he loved you when he never fucking did.

"This is ridiculous," your dad says.

"*Nuestro hijo nos necesita. Deje de apartarlo.*" You can't make out all the words because her Spanish is too fast. You pull your blade out and start carving into your forearm.

"I'm calling the cops," your dad says through the door. "You're not staying in my house until you confess. Please forgive him, Father."

"Leviticus 20:13." As the priest says the verse on the other side of the door, you mouth the words along with him, leaning back on the headboard of your bed and closing your eyes. You know this one by heart. "If a man also lie with mankind, as he lieth with a woman, both of them have committed an abomination: they shall surely be put to death; their blood shall be upon them."

You hear your mom start crying, speaking too quickly in Spanish to your dad who's on the phone. He's actually calling the cops.

"Do you want the whole city to know what has happened here?" she says. You hear the phone click.

"If we confess our sins, he is faithful and just to forgive us our sins and to cleanse us from all unrighteousness," Father Mathus says. "John 1:9."

You call Isaac's phone and listen to his voice on the machine. You leave it on the end of the bed, so he can hear your mom banging on the door, screaming in Spanish to open up because it's her house. If he doesn't understand what he's done to you, he will now.

The left wrist is more difficult than the right one, now that it's bleeding—it's a slower cut. Everything in you feels weak, almost light. It's ending. Finally, it's ending.

The door rattles in its frame and you start feeling dizzy. But before you let it take you, you force yourself to stand. You hunch over to get your bearings before shuffling through your drawers for a piece of paper.

"This is your chance, John. This is your wake-up call. Right now," Father Mathus says, still using his sermon voice. "Romans 12:21. Do not be overcome by evil, but overcome evil with good."

You hesitate, but it's too late now. It's already done. You find a stubby pencil on the floor and start writing, using the blade as a flat surface. You have to keep wiping blood off the paper.

You leave the note on the window and lay back down on the bed, suddenly tired and extremely thirsty. You let their voices fade and spread your arms wide, watching your blood slowly slide down the folds of the sheets, pooling warm and smooth in your hands. Your only regret is that you wish you could see their faces when they find the note.

*This is the window I used to sneak out of to meet him. This is the window he snuck into so we could fuck while the two of you slept. - J*

You almost want to laugh, but you close your eyes instead. You've lost so much blood, you couldn't even remember his name.

The End

**Y**OU'RE GOING TO DO THE HONEST THING, EVEN IF IT ISN'T THE RIGHT thing—and it's definitely not the smart thing— but you're not going to make yourself Isaac's enemy.

"I don't have to do anything with a slut like you," you say to Mariana.

The crowd doesn't like that. You can practically feel it coming up from the grass and through your feet.

She crosses her arms. "So, you are queer."

"I say we help them find God," Lucy says. "What do you guys think?" The crowd responds neutrally, but that doesn't stop Lucy, who walks toward you and bundles up one hand in your shirt. Before you can process what he's doing he punches you hard in the face, making your head tight with pain. It feels like something splits right behind your eyes. You try to keep yourself standing, but you have to lean.

"Stop!" Isaac tries to push himself between you and Lucy, but he shoves him off, still holding you straight. Someone needs to get him out of here.

"Let's see if I can kill two fags at once," Lucy says. There's nothing you can do to stop him from throwing you on the ground next to the fire pit. You've lost your balance.

Isaac leaps up and swings forward, clipping Lucy in the jaw with his scrawny arm. He lunges toward Isaac like a bull, tackling him to the ground almost on top of you. Mud gets kicked up from their sneakers in the grass and Lucy's straddling him, hitting him across the cheek over and over while you stand up. Isaac's neck moves unnaturally and blood is all over his mouth.

You grab him around the shoulders and pull back, only now noticing the crowd going insane, cheering for blood in the flickering light thrown by the fire. You use your momentum to pull him backwards, but he lands on you, elbowing you in the stomach. He turns quickly and punches you, not in the face, but in the stomach again, then the chest, knocking the wind out of you. You put your hands up to surrender but he hits you in the chest again, harder. You can't breathe.

Suddenly Lucy yelps in a thin voice you've never heard from him before, whimpering like an abused animal. You look up to see Isaac yanking his elbow back. Lucy jerks and curls, brushing over you before dropping to the grass, squeezing his arms over his belly while Isaac puts his hands up like he's trying to surrender, dropping a knife. Your knife. He must have grabbed it from your pocket when he fell by you.

"Oh, shit," someone says.

You turn your face against the dirt. Lucy's only breathing in, and only with tiny gulps. Isaac pulls you up before you realize it's him. At first you try to fight him off.

Mariana screams, "Call 911!" She's trying to work her own phone, but seems too drunk to unlock it.

Isaac looks closely at you, like he's trying to see what he did through your reaction. "I had to. He was going to kill you. You saw him, Jay. I had to."

"This is my fault," you say. You want that look off of his face. You want to turn back time. "Not yours, Isaac. Don't worry." You try to put your arm around his shoulder but the movement seems to make him alert. He looks you dead-on and serious.

"Don't follow me." His voice is shaking. He's scaring you now.

"Where are you going?"

He backs away and moves through the crowd that opens up to make room for him like he has a disease. You can't tell if Lucy's alive or dead. "Isaac!" you yell but he's already running. You can see the white stripe of his jacket in the moonlight before it disappears in the trees.

No one pays attention to you anymore. No one gives a shit. You walk toward the tree line where you last saw him. The woods are quiet.

"Isaac!" You hope he's close, hiding out, but

there's no answer. He's probably still running. "Come back! We can fix this!"

When you get no reply you call him on your phone, jogging through the woods. You feel sick when you hear his voicemail.

Forty minutes later, you walk toward the place you've been avoiding, still shaking from the image of him with your knife. It doesn't seem possible. A part of you liked seeing Lucy suffer. You try to force the thought away but it keeps coming back. You liked seeing him hurting. You need to stop thinking. Isaac. *No piensas en el.*

You stand in line at a food drive for the home-less, skirting around people's tents and garbage bags of belongings, among mostly older men and women with missing teeth, but you don't see him.

Once you get your food you sit down at one of the tables in the auditorium to think about where he could have gone. You sleep out in the open between two tents, a poor kid even here. But he doesn't show up.

The first day at school after the incident, you find out Isaac put Lucy in a coma. You're left to deal with Lucy's friends until they find out whether Lucy will live or die from the lack of oxygen in his brain. Lenny glares at you and crosses himself in class before pushing you over in the halls. "This is your fault. Your fucking boyfriend is going to pay for what he did. In this life or the next." Mariana yells at you in Spanish if you ever come near her.

For the next few weeks, you call him every day but he never answers. The comments get worse as Lucy gets worse. You're sent to detention twice over the past three weeks because of fights with Lenny. You lost both of them, choosing to run.

One day you decide to just stop going. It isn't worth the trouble.

You sleep at the shelter for the rest of the school year. You try calling your parents, but they won't talk to you, won't even give you a chance to say you could be straight if you wanted to.

You feel yourself cutting closer and closer to the vein.

One day you get a text from a random number with a Sacramento area code and you almost cry from how much you love him. He's alive.

*Find me. Te amo.*

That night you pack whatever belongings you have left, barely anything at all, really, and go over who you might say goodbye to before you leave, but there is no one. You take the Greyhound to a house in Sacramento.

You have to check the address twice, because the place looks abandoned. There's a lawnmower turned on its side out front, the windows are boarded up, and the roof is just plywood, no shingles.

The door opens before you even want to knock. Isaac lunges for you and holds you on the porch. You feel like you're about to cry until you part and see what you've been holding. Isaac's hair is longer than ever, all the way past his shoulders and greasy, barely covering how skinny he's gotten, how skeletal his face is. His eyes are almost closed and he has some kind of rash on his neck—his cross necklace is gone.

"Do you have money?" he asks.

"What happened to you?" you ask. He pulls you inside where there's a white guy with patchy hair smoking something on the couch. "What is this?"

"This is Ben," he says. It sounds like he hasn't used his voice in a long time. "He's helping me pay rent. He's gay too. He gets it. You know?"

"Have you talked to your parents?"

"No. I can't." He shakes his head, almost like a twitch or a shiver. "Did you bring money?"

"That's why you brought me here? Money?"

Isaac sits down with the other guy and picks up a bong from the coffee table. You wonder if he's how Isaac's been paying for whatever else he's on. "Did I kill him?"

You look at the guy on the couch. He doesn't seem fazed by the remark. Ben looks like he's probably done worse. If you tell Isaac that Lucy woke up from the coma a week ago, he'll want to go back.

He'll want to try again to make a life in that fucking nightmare. You can't even walk down the streets in Escondido without being terrified of getting jumped by some of Lucy's friends. They don't blame you for Lucy. They blame you for being a fucking faggot.

"Yeah," you say. "Lucy's dead."

You sit next to him and try to make him put the bong down so you can hold his hand. He looks at you like you disgust him and yanks it back. You already feel like you need the blade again, but you shake it off. "Come with me, Isaac. I'll get you better."

"We're going to Hell, Jay."

You swallow down the guilt before looking around at what's going to be your new home and you wonder if you are already in Hell.

No. This isn't the end. You'll pick up the pieces of him just like he picked up the pieces of you in Escondido. You just can't be scared anymore. You'll get Isaac sober and away from this creep. As long as you're together and he never finds out the truth, you'll make this work. That's how much you love him.

"You know, it doesn't feel so good," he says, startling you out of your thoughts. "It doesn't feel so good what you do. It doesn't help me at all, Jay."

You watch his eyes jumping around before you understand. You take both of his hands in yours and turn his wrists, remembering the night in the park before your birthday. There aren't as many scars and cuts on his arms as yours, but they aren't calm, slow ones either. He did these high on something hard, not weed—making jagged, angry slices down his forearms.

"Isaac, listen—"

"I missed you," he says quickly. "What took you so long?"

The End

# 10

FOR THE LAST FEW WEEKS BEFORE YOU LEAVE FOR CAMP, YOU FEEL FREE to say anything you want to Father Mathus during your little counseling sessions. It's a new feeling, a good one. There's nothing to lose anymore. When you speak up, you feel a release similar to cutting. The thoughts in your head stop being wild, uncontrollable—they become manageable.

"It's not having an attraction to men that is sinful, it's acting on that whim that constitutes the sin. The camp is meant to help you deal with this initial inclination and act on a—"

"Straighter path?" you say, leaning back.

"No jokes, John. Your sexuality is a choice, no

matter how you see it. It will help you learn to consistently make better ones."

"It's not a choice. Even if it were, doesn't free will mean anything?"

Since you've been more honest, he's started pacing behind his desk during his interrogations. "Do you remember the last time you felt an attraction to a woman?"

"I never did."

"I find that very hard to believe."

"I tried. I thought that I could at least fake it for a while, but it's just not who I am."

He sits down. "When did you realize that you were attracted to men?"

"When did you realize you were attracted to women?" you return. He glares at you. He hates it when you don't answer a direct question.

"Have you had any more dreams about Isaac?"

You shake your head, looking at the pamphlet for Truth Sports Camp in his fingers. It's a place to help Catholic homosexuals control the urges that traumatic events from their childhood have left them with. Father Mathus keeps trying to find yours, trying to dig into your past to see at what point exactly did you get raped by five guys and were changed forever into a sinner.

"You're trying to narrow who I am down to single events and turning points—choices—"

"Is a person not the sum of their choices?" he says, obviously proud of himself.

"I don't think a person can be summed up." You smile. "Besides, no choice I make or have ever made is going to change the part of me that loves."

He tilts his head like he's sorry for you before giving you instructions for Hail Marys. You follow them, only feeling guilty for lying to God, if He's even there. If He hates you for what you are, you hate Him for what He is. Father Mathus has made that clear.

---

You drop your suitcase on the floor and announce, "Okay, I'm ready to go."

Your mom looks up from a book she's reading on the couch by the altar. It looks like the Spanish-to-English dictionary. Maybe she wanted to do something right for your dad now that there's no hope his son will. It's the Saturday after your high school graduation and your dad is out. "Good, *hijo*. When will you be back?"

"End of June," you say, wondering why you're suddenly scared. "Or as soon as I get better."

"Father Mathus has been telling me all about it. I'm glad you're opening up." She hugs you. "Are you sure you can't wait for your father to get back?"

"I already said goodbye to him," you say quickly, trying not to act jumpy like he'll walk in the door at any moment. You add the lie to the long list of things you have to cut yourself for tonight.

"I'm so proud of you." She squeezes you tighter. "We'll be a happy family again in no time. You'll see."

"*Te amo*," you force yourself to say. "I'll miss everyone."

"It won't be long." She lets you go and you grab

your suitcase off the floor. She gives you the money you need to pay for the camp. "You sure you have to pay there?"

"Yeah," you say, trying not to think about the fact that this was probably at least part of your college money. They would sacrifice your college education to make you straight. You're suddenly not sorry for running anymore. "Thanks."

You take one last look at your house and when you finally get outside, you flip it off, hoping the neighbors are watching you through their windows. When you drop your hand, you shiver. You're cutting all ties.

You sleep most of the way to Redding and daydream about your new life for the rest of the trip. You barely get inside the motel room before dialing Isaac's number, but he doesn't pick up. You try two more times that night, but again, no answer.

It takes two weeks to finally get a job at Diego's Restaurant, using your Spanish to get it. You like imagining how insulted your dad would be if he found out you would sink so low.

You call Isaac every day, but it takes him a few days after when camp was supposed to end for him to actually answer.

You're sitting by the chair against the window of your motel, fiddling with your knife. For two weeks you've stopped cutting yourself by thinking of Isaac showing up at your door. You stop twirling it and grip the handle tight when you hear his voice.

"John, where the hell are you?"

"Isaac," you say, startled. His name feels good. "I'm in Redding."

"Is that where the camp is? Why didn't you come back? Your parents asked me where you are." His voice should calm you down, but it just makes you nervous.

"I didn't go to the camp, I came here so that you and I could live together and get out of that town. If you'd just answered earlier we could've been living together for the past two weeks."

There's a pause that makes your shoulders feel heavy. Your heart beats faster as you wait for him to talk. "I can't go up there," he finally says. "What the hell were you thinking?"

"But we always planned this—"

"My life is here, John. I know high school was shitty and this town is a nightmare. That's why I wanted you here to help me get through it until we could leave at the right time, together. Not run away and hide before we even figure everything out here. My family is here."

"When do you think you can come?"

"I'm going to college early this summer, not next fall. Penn State."

You stand up and pace the room, flipping your knife open again. You barely finished high school, your grades were always shit anyway, and you have no money. You're not going to college and you are definitely not going to Penn State. You probably couldn't even afford to visit him. "So what you're saying is I did all of this for nothing because you never meant any of it in the first place?"

"We were always going to go to college together, not

run away together. And don't forget the last time we talked you basically told me to fuck myself, so I guess this is my chance to send that message back to you."

"Do you even know where I've been? I've been in the fucking hospital, going to the fucking church every day. Please, Isaac, I'm really trying—"

"You should come back while you still can. We can help each other here. We'll keep each other safe."

You remember the look on your mom's and dad's faces when you told them you were gay, and how it stayed even after you started lying that you weren't. You remember Father Mathus making sure you say the Hail Marys the correct number of times. Standing over you every afternoon like some kind of divine conscience. You think of the people, people you don't even know, who hate you just for what you are.

"I can't go back. I'm safe here," you say. You ran away to begin a new life. One where you can be anyone you want to be. You can be John or Juan, gay or straight—it doesn't matter. You can make your own decisions now. With Isaac out of the picture, you won't ever be anchored to who you were, where you came from. You can choose what's right and what's wrong. You can love who you want to love. "I saved myself," you finally say.

"And left me here alone." He sighs, angry. "I'm not running from my life because I'm scared. I'm dealing with it. You should too."

He hangs up before you can answer, but you answer anyway, wanting to hear the words out loud. "I will," you say. "I will take care of myself."

You sit back in the chair, the knife still in your hand, and know that pointing the blade down into the meat of your thigh will take this feeling away. There will be no future, no past, no John, no Juan, or Jay, just a single, throbbing pain. You're not sure you are ready to let this feeling go. You close the knife, studying your initials, and know, somehow, you'll survive.

The End

# 11

YOU WALK TOWARD THE BLACK SILHOUETTE OF THE CROSS ON THE ROOF of the church, sideways against a blue sky. The church doors are never locked. Some kind of metaphorical thing, probably, but in the end it's practical. Homeless people congregate there at night, especially in the winter. To them, the church is just a roof.

The pews are close together and the seats have high enough backs to hide you while you sleep. When you step inside, your hands start shaking. You turn away from the stained glass window in the back and try not to look at the candles and crosses holed up in the walls. You're about to break down again now that everything has died down. The feeling of being a traitor comes back, sitting heavy on your shoulders.

You stop when you hear noise. A giggle by the front of the room.

"Hello?" Your voice echoes.

"I am the messenger of God." Whoever it is tries to make his voice deep and booming. "I've been chosen!" A group of people start laughing and shushing him. He says, "I have," like he really means it.

You walk down the middle aisle toward five people sitting on a blanket on the floor between pews. They have needles, spoons.

"Hey," an old woman with short red hair says pleasantly. Her voice is slow from the heroin. Somehow she's feeling good, not thinking. Thinking gets you in trouble. Thinking makes you say his name.

You ask, "*Puedo?*"

A woman with black, frizzy hair next to her starts shaking her head frantically, but the one with red hair pats the blanket next to her. "Here," she says, her voice light and inviting. You sit on the floor. You ask how it works. The man with a thick black beard and mustache leans over to you and whispers, "They don't believe me. You believe me, don't you?"

"Don't listen to him. He thinks he's God or something."

"How do you know he isn't?" says the red-haired lady. "We're all God, aren't we?" They argue for a while, but you try to block them out and pay attention to how injecting heroin works—it's scientific, calculated, each person in that room serious and concentrating despite their teeth falling out and the smell of piss on the blanket. When the needle goes in, their necks snap back and their mouths open as if they're in awe. When you do it, you like the pain of the needle as it enters your arm. You even like the fear you feel when you rise up to the ceiling and float there, your mouth dry and your whole body warm.

This is better than not thinking. This is not being alive.

"Want to see something cool?" you feel yourself ask.

"No, *I* have something cool," says one of them. You can't keep track of them anymore.

You flip open the blade of your knife, pull your shorts up so your thigh is exposed, and point the knife down. You push in and feel your breath catch somewhere up high in your mouth, but you keep quiet through the pain. You focus.

"Holy shit," someone says.

You can hear the pleasant voice of the red-haired lady. "How do you feel? Does that feel good?" She sounds curious, like it's some new drug for her to try. Hell, it pretty much is. It's just as addicting.

You make the line a curve and the blood comes out and drips down. Feeling the pain while floating on this drug makes it feel kind of far away, like it's happening to someone else.

"What're you making, man?" says one of the other two sitting behind everyone. They look younger than the rest. A boy and a girl, leaning on each other. Probably together.

You look between the two of them, the girl

running her fingers on his arm. "Do you believe in God?" Your voice feels like it's bouncing off the walls.

"We're here, aren't we?" the woman says. You watch her eyes to see what she means exactly, but she's staring at your knife.

"He's fucking insane."

"I told you not to call me that." The older guy starts crying.

You push harder, the pain cold through the warmth of the blood.

"J?"

"Yeah, J, dipshit. I can read."

"C. J. C."

One guy starts cracking up, a high pitched noise. "He's a fucking religious nut. That's what it is."

"Hey, you gonna save us?"

"No, I am. I'm the messenger."

"We are all God. There is no message. We are the message."

"You know what, like, what if he, like, does. You know? What if this is it? For all of us?" It must be the young girl, since you haven't heard her voice yet. You're too concentrated on making the letters to look up and your head feels too heavy, anyway. You feel too good to stop.

"Shut up," the young guy says back to her.

You're about to finish with the G but you decide it's better to give these people something to believe in. This town is gossip, blind faith, lies. When you look back on your work, it's not enough. You slice down as hard as you can and something sharper pinches deep in your thigh and you're suddenly bleeding too much. You've never bled like this before, but all you can do is stare at it. You feel glued to the floor.

"I didn't mean to do that," you say sleepily. You don't think anyone noticed. You look down at the blood running down the side of your leg. You think you can see your pulse, but you can't be sure what's real.

"Dude, he's gonna bleed out in here. We're gonna get in trouble."

"Did we do that?"

"Nah, it's not us. You saw him. Besides, this ain't our church."

"It's *my* church. *I'm* the messenger."

"I'm not going to jail if he dies."

"We're all going to Hell. Oh God, we're all going to Hell."

You mumble again, "I didn't mean to do that."

"Shhh. I want to hear what he says."

"Shhh." It's like they're all saying it at once, all of their toothless faces leaning over you. "Sssshhhh!"

You suddenly don't recognize where you are. An empty building with voices. You try to swallow but your throat feels closed up. You can't focus. The voices stay quiet to hear you. "Isaac?" you whisper.

"There's your fucking message, Kylie."

"What? But that doesn't mean anything. It's just a name."

"Isaac."

There's one more chuckle as the group exits the church, leaving you on the blanket, and then silence once the door swings shut.

The End

# 12

AT NIGHT, EL DORO HIGH SCHOOL LOOKS AS SHITTY AS IT DOES IN THE daylight, but the windows are dark, the gate on the fence is padlocked, and even the lights beneath the announcement board are dim. You shudder at the cold but keep walking toward the squat buildings just behind the fence. You're pretty sure you can sleep in the gym if you can get in. You'll just have to wake up before school starts so no one finds any new reason to make fun of you.

You shove your sneakers in the holes of the fence and climb over, tripping on the cement border just beyond it. You pull the hood of your jacket over your head, just in case.

You make your way down the familiar walkways until you get to the backside of the gym where there's a window so high up no one ever shuts it. Luckily there isn't any trash in the dumpster near it, so you pull it over and climb through, but the noise probably wakes up everyone from here to the park.

The landing shoots bullets up your feet when you hit the floor and the sound echoes off the walls. You pull over one of the heavy wrestling mats beneath the window for a bed. You hope the sun will wake you up tomorrow so Isaac doesn't find you like this, curled up on the floor. You hope your parents miss you so that it'll mean something when you don't come back.

Lights from cars passing along the road cast shadows from one end of the room to the other. You watch them for a while until they pass by less and less. It must be late. When you open your phone you see you have three missed calls from your parents. You chuck it across the room and hear it slide over the hardwood floor.

You're too hungry to sleep. Isaac, your mom and your dad, your grandparents, even your little cousin who looked at you like he didn't know what the word "gay" meant—their faces keep flashing in your mind. You've ruined so many people's lives because you couldn't keep one fucking secret, not even until the end of the school year.

No, Isaac was the one who couldn't keep your secret. Isaac put you here. You sigh, trying to believe it.

You hear birds chirping, a shout from outside. The whole room is lighter and the dark blobs from last night are a weight machine, a trashcan, and a basketball cage. You get up quickly and head to the door. Before you leave, you look through the narrow gym windows on the doors. No one there. Just dew from being up so early.

Thankfully, the doors still open from the inside, and while the thought of actually attending class feels ridiculous, you don't know what else to do. When school starts, you go.

You spend the next few days living off your extra

meal tickets from the school cafeteria. At night you wait outside, sometimes wander downtown, sometimes even creep up on your own apartment building, though you never see anyone. At the end of the third day your phone battery dies.

On the fourth day, you get your name blared through the speakers to come to the office. When the secretary holds the phone out to you, you take it and speak quietly. They wouldn't even come here in person.

"What do you want?"

"*Ay dios mio.*" Your mom starts speaking Spanish so quickly that you can't pick up on it.

"I'm fine. I'm—staying at a friend's house for a few days," you say. You can hear her sigh waver on the other end. "What does Dad have to say?"

She takes a while to answer. You pace back and forth quickly in the far corner of the room. "He doesn't want you coming back here."

"What?"

"We just want what's best for you."

You hang up, ignoring the secretary yelling when you slam the door behind you.

When Isaac shows up in your English class, you can only manage to stare at the dark circles under his eyes. You catch someone shoving him in the hallway, but you keep moving. You've never seen him look so defeated, but you guess that's what he deserves. You shouldn't protect someone who won't protect you.

You start saving food from the cafeteria instead of eating it, but once the weekend hits, you down it all Saturday morning and are hungry again by dinnertime. By midnight you feel like you're going to pass out from exhaustion. You wander back over the fence from your usual walk down Clark Street and approach the gym, but a noise catches you off guard. You stumble behind the dumpster under the window before seeing Lucy, Mariana, Lenny, and three other assholes from your school. It looks like they have spray paint and a backpack probably full of something illegal. You hold your breath but it's too late.

"Hey, faggot," you hear. Lucy smiles as you step out to meet them.

"I was just leaving."

"Don't act like you don't know," Lenny says too loudly. One of his friends grabs you by the shoulders. "You're outed, motherfucker. How does it feel knowing Isaac told everyone your little secret?"

You try to keep eye contact with him and keep yourself from asking more questions or sounding angry. That will only make it worse. "I'm not gay."

"Who would you rather fuck? Me or him?" one of the taller guys says, gesturing to a pudgy kid with long blonde hair. The group laughs. You try to break out of the guy's grip on your shoulders, but you can't.

"You guys know he's gay," Lucy says.

They laugh. One guy says, "Obviously. Look at his hair."

"Well, poor John doesn't know it," Lucy says,

turning back to you. Mariana is smoking a cigarette next to him, not saying anything, but not looking at you, either. Lucy suddenly punches you in the gut, sending the air out of your chest. You cough from somewhere deep under your ribs, trying to get your voice back.

"Are you gay, man?" the pudgy one says, laughing. "Answer us."

"Are you?"

"Admit it."

"No," you manage to choke out.

"*Joto*," Mariana says. She puts her elbow up on Lucy's shoulder and looks down on you.

"Just admit it and we'll leave you alone," Lucy says.

One guy starts laughing. "Yeah, just tell us the truth, *compadre*." He tilts his head and emphasizes each word, slowly. "Are. You. A. Fag?"

You swallow hard as the group gets closer. You can feel the weight of your blade in your pocket, but what would that do? Make you a murderer? One of them smiles and the other two mumble to each other. Mariana and Lucy won't break until you do. Who are you going to be, John, Juan, Jay, whoever you are? Which one is it, anyway?

"Fine." You say it so quietly, it barely makes a sound. You're somehow, briefly, relieved. All your different selves are pulled together and it only took one word.

"He admits it!" Someone shoves your shoulder from the right. You didn't even see him. "You're dead fucking meat, queer."

You try to keep him at arm's length by grabbing his shirt but he overpowers you easily, swinging you to the ground.

"Get off of me!" you scream. You try pulling him one way or the other but he's massive and just sneers at you. He pulls his arm back but you manage to stop it using both hands before he can punch you in the face. The guy pins one of your arms down so he's free to hit you.

"Alright. That's enough," Mariana says at the

same time the guy gets enough backswing to punch you right up against your jaw, making your teeth knock against each other. He hits you again in the eye and you feel the cement slam against the back of your head as he does it. Your face feels numb and huge, swelled up already. You can't make yourself open your eyes again, and when you try, the guy laughs. His weight lifts and you want to sit up but you can't. All you can do is groan and cover your face, tasting the blood in your teeth.

Then everyone else joins in. All of them take turns hitting you and you would think after a while you wouldn't be able to feel their shoes in your gut or against your head, but you feel it every time and hug yourself into a ball on the ground. If you tried to get up, you'd only make them hit harder. You're in surrender mode, and the embarrassment of it, the feeling of helplessness is almost worse than the pain.

You curl tighter and only peek out to see if anyone at all isn't joining in, but everything is blurry. You hope to God you're not crying but you can't be sure. You're starting to get confused about things. You're not sure if you're screaming or laughing or crying or if they are. You should have run.

You start sliding along the ground and you feel like you're falling, like the earth tilted. You open your eyes and two people have your arms and are pulling you on your back across the pavement toward the front of school. You struggle to get out of their grasp but your movements are so small and every one of them hurts so you stop. You wait for what's next.

You're being forced to stand. You almost fall forward again when your legs feel broken, but a bunch of hands catch you.

"Whoa, buddy. Stand like a good boy."

"There you go."

You're up against something thin and cold and you feel something tight across your legs, then your stomach, then your shoulders, pressing on the bruises. It sounds like duct tape unrolling. Finally you find your voice.

"Hey," is all you can say and even that hurts. You're starting to feel everywhere they hit you. You have a headache that fills up behind your eyes and your throat. It's like something is broken in every part of you and all you want to do is lie down or tear someone's throat out, but you can't do either.

You try to glare at them, but you find yourself taking long blinks. You might pass out tied to the flagpole in front of school like a fucking moron.

"Ta-da! Now you're standing up all on your own."

All you can manage is a groan. You try to focus on them but your head sags and you can't relax all the way or the tape catches your neck and makes you gag.

"One last thing! Gimme that."

A cold hand slams the back of your head against the pole and there's cold pressure on your forehead. They're writing something there. You try one last time to get out but you start seeing spots.

"Okay. Okay, shit," Mariana says. You hear

voices far away and look one more time at them as they all back away. Lucy is holding the pen.

"Have a wonderful night, eh?" Lucy says and skips off toward the rest of the group.

Mariana stays and tears the tape on your throat loose. "In case you pass out," she says.

You're just angry enough to speak. "Why?"

She takes one last look at you. "We love who we love, don't we?" She moves out of your line of sight and their voices die down.

You try to pull yourself out or slide down but your knees won't bend.

"Fuck you," you say, but all you can do is put your lips together and open them again. The noises you make sound pathetic, so you stop. You want to be saved, but then again, you don't. You can't be found like this. You're not a fucking animal. You're not a pussy.

You struggle to get out again and again as the night wears on. Sometimes you think you hear them coming back and you're almost hopeful you could convince them to let you go, but they never come. At some point you start praying. You go over Mariana's words in your head until slowly they sink in, slowly you realize that the only reason you've been blaming Isaac is because you thought if you could find a way to hate him, you'd stop loving him.

When morning comes, a teacher you don't recognize shrieks and drops her car keys. She grabs your face and starts rubbing her thumb across your forehead. "They're gonna pay for this," she says. "I promise. What's your name?" She waits, then says, "Never mind, we'll figure out the details later. I'm calling an ambulance, okay? Let's get you out of this first. Where does it hurt? Who did this?"

She wouldn't stop talking and asking questions long enough for you to answer any of them, but you don't want to anyway. She drives you all the way to the hospital, making your phone calls for you, because you can't seem to breathe right. You rub your forehead, but nothing comes off in your palm.

The teacher tells you to stop, but you don't. You keep rubbing as hard as you can until it hurts and everything around you—the road, the church, the cemetery—blurs in your eyes.

No matter how many times the doctors ask you what happened—though you think they'd be able to tell—you keep your head down and tell them nothing. "It's fine," you keep repeating. "Just wash this off, please." You don't know how soon your parents will be here—you shock everyone who passes you. The word is finally out: you've been labeled what you really are—*Joto*.

Finally, a nurse rubs the word off with a bit of alcohol on a pad. You're exhausted but they keep you up in case you have a concussion. Trying to stay awake only makes everything worse, the anticipation for when your parents will show up even more painful.

Your mom shouts, "*Hijo!*" too loud and your dad keeps looking back and forth between you and the cops and the doctors, like he can't comprehend any of it. It's like he's following whatever your mom's doing.

"It's nothing—"

"I heard what happened," your mom says, grabbing your hand in both of hers. She isn't wearing makeup and she looks tired. She's been crying. You wonder if she and your dad got into a fight about whether or not they should come. "It's okay, I know."

You look at her hand holding yours. You think she must not know the whole story, but then she reaches up and touches your head, rubbing her thumb gently on your forehead. Behind her, your dad looks down, arms crossed.

"It's really true, then." You look up at your dad and you don't know how to read the expression on his face. "You'd rather get yourself killed than change?" Your mom shushes him. "Not now, *amor.*"

You didn't realize that was the choice you made—but now it's clear. You can't be John and Juan and Jay. There's only one of you, and he can't hide or it'll be the end of all of him. "I don't have a choice," you say quickly, almost whispering.

Your mom asks immediately, apparently prepared for the question. "Do you believe in God?"

Somehow the question makes you tear up again, and you nod. Tied to that pole—you prayed. You're shocked when your mom pulls you into a hug that you can barely move in. She glances behind her at your dad, whispering over and over, "That's all that matters to us. Right?" He drops his arms. "Please," she says. "This is our choice, too. He almost died today. Would you rather have him dead?"

She can barely say it without tearing up. He shakes his head and steps out the door and down the hall. Your mom touches your cheek again before going to find him.

---

You stay in the hospital for a few days, during which your story gets spread like the plague. The police keep mentioning a hate crime, which it is, you're sure of it. You saw the hate in Lucy's eyes that night. You can't forget how righteous he must've felt. In the hospital, your mom never leaves your side and your dad keeps people out of the room. He does this without speaking to you, without looking at you, until one day a camera crew from the local news actually shows up. When you tell him you don't want to do it, he ignores you. He tells you it's your duty, looking sad in his eyes, looking desperate. You don't understand it—he would never want this publicized—but he won't budge.

The hospital makes an interesting setting for the news story. Your mom smoothes your hair back and your dad puts on his work shirt to advertise his appliance company. They tell your story to the blonde news lady, who nods like she's concerned, like she knows what you've been through. She talks about the derogatory word written on your forehead without having to say it, then about how you got a broken rib, two black eyes, and about how long the road to recovery will be. Then she turns to your dad.

"How did you feel when you found out what happened to your son?"

You wince. There's only one answer to that and he can't say it on TV.

"You don't know how scary it is," he says. You look at him, confused. He adjusts himself in his seat and clears his throat. His eyes are wet. "To have someone you love in danger."

He glances at you only briefly, but it's long enough for you to wonder at his meaning. The interviewer smiles gently, giving the appropriate amount of respectful silence before turning to you. But you're distracted by your dad, hands folded in front of him like he's in prayer. He never hated you. All he ever wanted was to keep his family safe, and God was the only thing in this country, in his life, that he thought could do it. He was scared for your soul.

"And how do you feel about the people who did this to you?"

Reluctantly, you pull your eyes from your dad. "I don't know—" Your mom is squeezing your fingers while you try to form the words. Your dad is trying to look tough, get his dignity back. The interviewer nods for you to continue. You try to think of a way to explain it—you've had a lot of time in the hospital to piece it all together, a lot of time that night while you were strapped to that pole alone, feeling pain worse than any cut you've ever made, to wonder at the reasons for it. "It's like saying the same thing in two different languages. There's some very small people who have been taught their language is the right one, the only one."

She tilts her head. You try to block out your parents. Focus.

"But there is no right language, no right love, you know?" You pick at your hospital robe, trying not to seem too cliché. "It's all love. It's just—translated." You force yourself not to look up. "The people who attacked me don't like my language, but it's the one I speak. They can't understand it, even if we're both saying the same thing."

"So you understand their reasons. But do you forgive them?"

You glance at your dad, who's watching your hands intently.

"Jesus teaches us about forgiveness," you say. "But I don't know. I'm not sure that I can just yet."

The interviewer nods, says a few closing words and shuts her notebook, thanking each of you before leaving. Your mom rubs your arm.

Your story is on the eleven o'clock local news that night. The next day the phone is ringing off the hook. Kids from school are texting you to see if you're all right or see if it's true. People who don't even know you are calling and writing letters to end this violence against queer youth. Everybody knows your secret. Mr. Alfaro is the first neighbor to show up on your doorstep asking questions and yelling at your dad about God's will.

"It was on TV, Mr. Alfaro. I can't kick him out after that interview. How would our neighborhood look? My family?"

Mr. Alfaro mutters something you can't hear.

"It's about sacrifice," your dad says as he shuts the door.

You step out from behind the wall, confused. You've been feeling braver, less tired. You're strong now. "That's why you wanted to do the interview?"

He sits in the armchair in the living room under the wall of crosses and turns on the TV, looking uncomfortable.

"It's my job to protect you in this life. I know now that it's yours to protect yourself in the next. I was wrong to risk one for the other."

"Can I ask you a question?" you say, finally. When he doesn't reply you continue, carefully. "If someone hurts you when they were trying to help you—what do you do?"

He squints hard at you. "Like you said to that reporter, God encourages forgiveness."

You nod, still looking at your feet, wondering how long this closeness will last between the two of you. "Hey, dad—"

"Get your homework done today," he says, waving his hand. "I'm serious."

You're homeschooled now, working off the computer you got with the money from viewer letters. He's still your dad. "Sure."

Other people show up, almost all neighbors, but your dad shoos them away. You barely leave your house, but when you do, people in the neighborhood can't look you in the eye, even Lucy and Mariana. You realize that through this fucked-up situation you have gained a power over them. All you have to do is pick up the phone and the cops would put them away for a long time. You even hear that they have stopped picking on Isaac at school and that the teacher that found you tied to the flag pole, Mrs. Robertson, founded a LBGT Club at El Doro, which sounds pretty cool, even if it only has one member.

You miss Isaac, you do. It doesn't matter if he outed you or not. You love him, and the only reason he did what he did, just like your family, is because he loves you. He just wants what's best for you. You need to learn forgiveness—for yourself and for everyone else. You haven't opened your knife since that night, but it takes a few days to build up the courage to even text Isaac. You apologize in as many different ways as you can. You should never have ignored his pain. You're in it together.

You're in your room the next night, flipping through a textbook, when something hits your window. Outside, Isaac stands just out of the street light. He raises his hand and smiles.

The End

# 13

YOU HAVEN'T SAID ANYTHING TO YOUR PARENTS FOR A FEW DAYS after telling them off about their scheme to fix you. Your mom keeps grabbing your hands and turning them this way and that to make sure there aren't any new cuts. She doesn't know to look anywhere else.

You hear your parents arguing in harsh whispers about you in the living room. If you can still hear them in a few hours, if you can't sleep, you'll cut yourself again. The crosshatch of scars and scabs on your shoulders are making the crisp lines blur, the thickening tissue turns your skin a deeper shade of brown. It makes you want to die all over again, only this time the fantasy doesn't scare you. For the first time, it seems peaceful.

"*Hijo*," your mother says, relieved every time you open the door to your room after she's been knocking on it for half an hour, pleading with you to eat and please talk to them. You guess the only thing worse than having a gay son is having a dead son.

You catch your dad speaking to Sarah and Mr. Alfaro in a low voice one day. You watch them out on the breezeway, thinking they can't be heard.

"He's getting better. There's no need to worry anymore."

"Are you sure?" Sarah asks, looking back at the house. You lean up against the wall, listening.

"Everything is under control. We're sorry to worry you."

"We just want him to get better," Mr. Alfaro says. "This is a good community we have here."

"Don't worry. He's even applying to colleges. He's bright. Very bright."

You haven't looked either of your parents in the

eye since that day. Your dad makes sure he's on his way out when you come out of your room in the morning. He looks between you and your mom like he's waiting for something to happen. Then he says he's late for work and leaves. It's not what it's supposed to be like. Not talking for the past few weeks is supposed to be more satisfying.

Isaac either hangs up on you or you get sent to voicemail, but you keep calling, sometimes screaming at him, sometimes apologizing. Eventually you start telling him over voicemail about your day and about what you wish you'd be doing if you were together right now. You don't know where your real self is anymore now that cutting doesn't help as much as it did. Isaac will know how to find it for you again.

For the most part, you just want to know how he's doing—you know you hurt him. You end each voicemail asking him to see you, but he never answers or calls you back.

The next morning you wake up, get dressed in the purple shirt you know he likes, and walk out to the living room. Your mom is busy folding laundry on the back of the couch and your dad is watching TV. As usual, they don't notice you, or at least, pretend they don't.

When you get to school, you're going to show Isaac that you're serious about this. You don't believe in anything anymore except for the fact that you love him.

You see him in the parking lot outside in his car, scribbling on a piece of paper on the steering wheel, probably trying to finish his homework for first period. You move through the crowd toward him and open the passenger door. When you sit down, he just looks at you.

"What are you doing?"

"You know, I always thought you were an asshole, but I didn't realize how much of an asshole until now," you say.

"Get out of my car." He reaches over and opens the door for you, but you close it again.

"I mean, how can you change your mind so

suddenly about a person? How can you just turn your back on them when they need you?"

"I thought we were done talking about this. You made that pretty clear."

"Well, I'm not."

He looks at you now, sensing something familiar. This feels almost like you're at the park, messing with each other like you used to.

"Look, I'm just trying to protect you. If you have to pretend to be straight to stop hurting yourself, that's what you have to do."

"What if I wanted to be with you?"

He shakes his head. Something slams on the hood of his Jeep, shaking the whole thing. Lucy is leaning over it into the windshield.

"How's it going, guys?"

"This is what I'm talking about," Isaac says. "You want to deal with this? You want to be with me, you have to be with me through the shit, too."

"No. We can't do this anymore. Move," you say. You pull your feet up onto the seat, keeping an eye on Lucy,

Lenny, and the rest of their crew, who are knocking on the windows of the Jeep and talking to each other.

"What are you doing?"

"Let me drive," you say. You shove him part way out until he finally moves out of the seat into the passenger side. The car is already running. You put it in drive and release the brakes a little, making Lucy jump back with his hands up.

"Motherfucker," he says. "You gonna run me over, is that it?"

You step on the gas and Lucy falls on his back. You screech to a stop. Lenny bangs on the window. "What the hell, man?"

"Holy shit," Isaac says, gripping the dash with his fingers. "Okay, that's enough. You scared him."

"You want him to leave you alone, don't you?" you say. Lucy is standing now, a distance away from the car, but he made the mistake of going toward the stop sign by the road, instead of deeper into the school. You push on the gas and then the brakes. Lucy backs up.

"Oh, come on, man. Real mature," he says, but you can see he's scared. He knows the shit he puts Isaac through. He won't hurt him anymore.

You do it again, stepping on the gas and hitting the brakes. Lucy stumbles backwards and uses his fingers to push up from the cement and starts running. You pass him as close as you can. Behind you, students have stopped running to class. They've turned around on the front steps to watch.

"Stop! Jay, stop it! You're gonna fucking kill him!"

"I won't let him mess with us anymore. We're not his fucking playthings." You slam down on the gas as you turn, almost making you spin completely around to see Lucy now running the other way.

You wait for a long time, watching his run turn into a jog. He turns around and flips you off. That's when you step on the gas again, harder than before.

"Stop it! Shit!" Isaac says, grabbing your arm. Even now it makes your skin tingle. You missed him so fucking much.

"I'm gonna stop right in front of him. He'll be

scared of us this time." You're getting closer now. Lucy is running again, he turns the corner somewhere you can't see and when you make the turn, you didn't realize he had slowed down. You have to slam on the brakes just as Isaac grabs the wheel and yanks it the opposite direction and the Jeep crashes right into a fountain in front of the school, cracking the cement, smashing the front end, and sending a pole through the windshield.

Your ears ring and glass crunches in your teeth before you black out.

When you open your eyes. Isaac is leaning on a metal pole from a fence. You can't move at all. It takes a few minutes before you see the blood leaking from his shirt. You want to move your arm to shake him but nothing happens, your whole body is numb. The door is smashed into you, cradling you so you can't move.

It doesn't look like he's breathing.

The rest of the week goes by in a blur. You keep asking where he is, what's happening to him, but they've put so many drugs into your system you're not even sure what language you're speaking. When they finally do tell you—some doctor, not your parents, not Isaac's parents—you don't think you heard them right. It doesn't make any sense. It can't be real; he was just here, he was just alive. You had a whole future together, finally, after so much time, and now you're asking yourself questions you don't want to know the answer to. If it's true, what do you do now? How do you forgive yourself? You don't even remember if he was wearing his necklace. You can't remember if he believed in God when he died.

Something is so fucking wrong with you. You can't even cry. He is not gone. He'll come find you. He'll throw pebbles at your window when you least expect it.

You only see your mom and dad briefly when they sign your release papers from the hospital before they disappear. They don't answer when you call them collect from jail. Isaac's parents are the only ones who visit you in the county lock-up. Every time they do, something deep down hurts so bad that you hold your breath, like that will kill you, end this nightmare. If it wasn't for this single pane of glass separating you from them, they could beat you, strangle you, shoot you. You deserve everything. Some of the other inmates are happy to help. There's no place for a long-haired, eighteen-year-old Mexican gay kid to hide behind bars. You try and take your beatings like penance. You've been cutting yourself on whatever you can find in your cell, cutting deeper than you ever have, but it doesn't feel real. Nothing feels real.

They tell you from the jail's visitors' room that you'll be let out for the funeral.

"Where?"

His mom says it so quietly you're not sure you heard her right, "Saint Mary's."

You breathe out too fast and the guilt hits you so hard you wish something, anything would crush you. They let him in the church, even though they knew what he was.

"He really loved you," Isaac's dad says. You can tell he's been crying a lot and no one would blame him for that. "Here. This was Isaac's. We want you to have it."

You read it every day. When you reach the end you start over, looking out for the passages Isaac highlighted.

John 15:12-13: *My command is this: Love each other as I have loved you. Greater love has no one than this, that he lay down his life for his friends.*

John 3:18: *Let us not love with words or tongue but with actions and in truth.*

John 4:17: *Let us love one another, for love comes from God. Everyone who loves has been born of God and knows God.*

You read over those passages every night, like a prayer.

The End

# 14

YOU'RE GOING TO TRY TO ACCEPT THAT YOU DON'T KNOW WHAT'S BEST for you anymore. When you let them drive you to the support group for the first time, you feel numb. It's like you're not even anyone anymore.

"John." Your dad leans over your mom in the car and looks up at you. "I'll know if you're lying about going to this thing, got it?"

You nod—your body feels like someone else's, your thoughts are foreign—it feels like falling. If you live or die—that's up to them now. "See you soon, *hijo*," your mom says, before the Toyota drives off.

The support group meets in a recreational building where they have exercise and yoga classes on the weekends. Two hours a week you have to be here, staring at the ridiculous goatee on the man who leads the discussion. Everyone is standing off at the snack table by the door when you come in, Goatee Man sitting and chatting with an older black man who leans over him too close. One girl looks up at you from the paper cup she's holding, terrified. You try to smile, but she walks away.

The walls of the tiny room are a sickly-looking green. The chairs and tiny desks are scattered everywhere except for a makeshift circle of them in the corner. It looks like it's supposed to be a kindergarten classroom—there's an alphabet poster above one of the windows. Even the snack table covered with yellow and green cookies feels out of place—too cheery for people who want to kill themselves.

Everyone's still pretending, even your parents. They can still fake it like they're just dropping you off at the gym.

You see a familiar face huddled in a group between two other people. That's definitely your neighbor

Sarah's blonde hair and dark skin. If she knows you're here then she'll tell everyone in the neighborhood, and you'll be a joke again. Immediately, you turn your back to her. You take a step toward the door, but you hear a raspy voice say, "Welcome to the group, John." Goatee Man walks toward you, holding his hand out. You shake it as he says, "I'm sorry you couldn't make our first introduction session." The twelve-week program had already started, but your parents threw you into the mix anyway.

You shrug. "Sorry I didn't reach a breaking point at a more convenient time for you." He keeps holding the hand he was shaking and looks at you sympathetically.

"I'm sorry, John. I meant no offense." He lets you go when you don't break his gaze. Then he turns toward the rest of the room. "If it's okay with everyone else, let's get started."

Even though you try to look away, Sarah turns around and sees you. She doesn't wave or say anything, just looks at you with a sort of soft look in her eyes. You sit between a bigger guy probably in his thirties and a girl with short black hair who looks like she can't be more than fourteen. Sarah is across from you, next to Goatee Man, who introduces himself as Dr. Ruiz, but you can call him José.

He motions to you to introduce yourself first, since you're the new guy.

"My name is John Carlos Garcia." Everyone in the room greets you with a nod and a mumble. You look between each person, not sure if you should smile.

"And why are you here, today, John?" José asks. You shrug and shuffle your feet on the floor. He nods. "It's okay to tell the truth, even if you don't think it's the right answer for the purposes of this class. We're all about being honest, aren't we? Especially with ourselves. I would really appreciate it if you thought about why you want to be here before our next session—and not because of your parents or a counselor." A few people laugh, but you don't get what's funny. "Now, are you familiar with what this class is trying to accomplish?"

Sarah speaks up, reciting what you're sure is the whole mantra of the program, word for word. "I want to stop using self-injury to hurt myself physically, emotionally, mentally, and socially. I want to be honest with myself and others about my use of self-harm. Self-injury is a choice, and I want to be aware that every time I harm myself, it is a choice I am making. I am always capable of making the right one to keep myself safe."

"That's absolutely correct," José says. "And remember that our goal is to totally, one hundred percent, end our self-harm. There are no compromises or baby steps when it comes to healthy choices."

Everyone nods at once—you're in a room of brainwashed zombies who all found the same solution. You can see the scars on a few of them and familiar ways of hiding them on others. There are about ten in the class, and everyone tells when they started to self-harm, but only some of them go into detail about why.

The big guy next to you, for instance, only started cutting a few months ago, after he had to move back in with his parents when he got out of jail.

"Can't get a job, a girl, nothing. I just can't help feeling like a fat piece of shit when I look in the mirror. I'm just taking up space. The world would be better off without me."

Sarah talks about failing her classes, and the student loans she's taking out that she'll never be able to pay back. She says she never feels good enough. She won't sleep because she needs to study; she won't eat because she needs to work one of her two jobs, and she can't meet anyone new because there's no time, but what's the point because she'll just disappoint them anyway. She briefly mentions a boyfriend that "didn't work out" and looks away from the group.

Everyone feels worthless.

"I'm just a burden to my parents. They want me dead and so do I sometimes. When I cut myself, it feels right."

"I'm lonely. Every time I try to talk to one of my friends or family members it's like they don't even see me. So instead, I smile. I pretend like it's okay."

"My anxiety makes it hard to talk to anyone. I fake it like everything's normal, but I feel like I'm spiraling. I don't know how to stop thinking about killing myself."

"When I cut myself, I feel release. I can get over my insomnia for a while. I can get a good night's sleep."

The whole time they speak, you twirl your phone between your fingers and keep your eyes out the window. Everyone being so open about their feelings makes you uncomfortable—this isn't what you're used to. When José asks you when you started your self-harm, you don't know how to explain that if there's a problem in your family, you shove it under the rug and make sure the rug looks nice when people come over.

"I don't remember."

"Everyone remembers their first time," a young guy with blonde hair says and leans back.

"It's okay, John," José says.

"I said, I don't know. It was probably middle school."

"Puberty can be a very difficult thing to go through."

Puberty alone wouldn't have been so bad, but when everyone else your age started making obscene jokes and looking at pictures of naked women in magazines, you started to ask yourself why you weren't feeling what they were feeling. It was seeing how other people reacted that made you realize something was wrong with you. When they looked at you funny, you stuttered, said. "She's got nice tits, but I've seen better in real life."

The two boys you were with shoved you, saying, "No way, tell us." You made up a whole story, smiling the whole time, acting like you lost your virginity to some high school girl when you were twelve. Really, it was just information you got when you were looking up girls to try to understand what was happening to you. "Did you fuck her?" they asked.

"Yeah, I fucked her."

When they left, you found yourself trying to run your forearm along the edge of a butter knife. When it drew blood, it made up for your lie. You crossed yourself and thanked God for forgiveness—but it never felt like enough. After a month you stopped trying to fool yourself and brought the knife to your room. Something about it made you feel better.

That was the day you realized there are two versions of you: who you are, and who you should be. You'll spend the rest of your life trying to be the man you should be and hurting yourself when you don't live up to the image you have of your perfect self in your head, or in your parents head, or Isaac's, or God's. You were good at the balancing act until people at school started making comments. Until Isaac was your lab partner freshman year and he asked if you were gay after the last day of school and told everyone that he was. It started to feel like there were too many *you*s in one body, and they got hard to control.

"Yup," is all you can manage to say.

He lets the room settle, probably trying to get you to keep talking. The same guy who spoke earlier says, "How do you feel when you self-harm?"

"I don't know. I don't know if I feel anything."

"Yeah, sometimes that's the best part," he says.

Sarah leans forward. "It helps you stop thinking so much."

"If you focus on the pain, you can't focus on you." José folds his fingers in front of him, adding something now and then to keep the conversation going, but it fades off as the hour ends. José makes everyone hug at the end, which feels too cheesy for words, but when a few people start crying, you put your judgment aside.

The next few weeks go by the same way, with more and more of everyone's dark shit that ate away at them for so long suddenly bursting out at least once a session. Whenever there's some kind of epiphany like that, there's crying.

"Sadness is a necessity of happiness," José says once, which sounds more like a fortune cookie than advice, in your opinion. The crying didn't fix anything for anyone. For the most part, it seems like people are about the same week to week. But you guess they're still alive.

José's voice comes back to you. "This class will not fix all your problems at once. Its purpose is to help you help yourself, because at the end of the day, at the end of our twelve-week session, it's you alone with a knife and a choice. Depression is a mood disorder. I don't want you to look for cures. I want you to look for healthy outlets, healthy thought processes for controlling your desire to self-harm." He pauses for the effect of it. "It's going to take time and a lot of effort on your part to make the right choices. Just remember that your health and happiness is always worth it. We are all children of God."

When you go to school now, you avoid Isaac in the hallways, ignore when someone yanks his backpack off of his shoulders and dumps out his books over the ramp on Friday, and you ignore him when he gets pushed out of line in the cafeteria while someone calls him a fag. Everyone is still being harsher on him than you've ever noticed before.

They're being harsher on you too. You keep a tally in your notebook for every time someone calls you a fag or asks where your boyfriend is today. You would ask where they got the rumor from, but that would only make you look suspicious, make you look like you care. You stay quiet and accept the punishment coming to you.

The truth is, you know who started those rumors about you, in order to make you come out sooner. But then he met your dad and saw what it really means if you come out—getting the shit kicked out of you every day, having strangers hate you, having your parents hate you—and you'd end it, you'd kill yourself. Maybe he decided to spread these rumors for revenge after you yelled at him on your birthday. It doesn't matter. Either way, he betrayed you.

It's your new penance. You haven't cut yourself since the class started ten weeks ago. Your scars are there, but faded because you're confined by José's little speeches and your own paranoid, angry thoughts. You're constantly holding your breath, waiting for one of the two to win out.

It's better to have your parents think Isaac was just a bad influence. His sins have turned your mind away from God so strongly that you probably started cutting yourself the day you met him. They choose to think being sad is the problem because it's the easiest to swallow and the least embarrassing. They think they can fix sadness.

If you come out now, there's no point in keeping this stupid class going. You're only putting on this charade for José so your parents have an excuse for the way you acted at the dinner.

At the last session, everyone seems nervous. José reassures you that as long as you remember what you learned here, take responsibility for your choices, and stay on a healthy path, you will continue your progress. If you still need help, remember the next twelve-week session starts in a few days.

To come out to your parents, turn to page 24.

To continue the class, turn to page 178.

# 15

JOSÉ'S NEWEST HOMEWORK ASSIGNMENT IS TO OPEN UP TO SOMEONE outside of the support group. Sofia is the only person you could think of who might understand. When you ask if you can tell her something, she invites you to her house. You agree, because you might as well make sure it stays a secret between you and her by going somewhere private.

Once school ends, you find Sofia waiting for you in the parking lot by a silver Honda with a dent on the front bumper. She drives you to her place—a little two-room rental in the middle of town. When she parks, she says, "Looks like my dad's at work and my little sister's still at daycare. We have the place to ourselves."

"Yeah," you manage. "Great."

The walls are bare white, with one couch in the living room and no TV. She brings you to her room. One of the walls is purple, like she didn't finish painting it and there's a poster of some *Telemundo* pop star on the door when she closes it. You sit on the bed because there's no other furniture.

"Sorry about that," she says, gesturing to the poster. "I was a kid once, you know? So what are you going to tell me, John?"

It's different to talk about it in a group of other cutters. She's just a girl you were kind of friends with once. Maybe you shouldn't even tell her. It's not like José would ever know. "It's weird," you say.

"What?" she laughs. "Now I have to know."

"I mean, it's not funny. It's just weird to talk about it to you." You look back at her suddenly serious face and wonder what she's thinking. She sits down on the bed next to you and curls her legs beneath her. This isn't for José. "Okay, it's just this stupid homework assignment for my—class. It's like this support group, actually. And I have to tell someone that I cut myself so that I have something to talk about in the next session or something. So there it is."

She looks confused, but she doesn't back away. "What do you mean you cut yourself? Like, *cut*-cut yourself? Like, 'cause you're sad or something?"

You shrug. "I guess. It's not a big deal. My parents are making me go."

"Shit, John." She sits silently for a second, then reaches over to grab your hand. She holds on to it and rubs her thumb over yours.

"It's not a big deal," you say after the silence gets too long and you realize you were staring at your hands together. "They just wanted me to tell someone outside of the group, like, as an exercise. So, thanks."

"John?" She looks down at your hands twined together before breaking away from you. She takes your sleeve in her fingers and tries to push it up.

"What are you doing?" you whisper and pull away.

"Sorry." She puts her hands in her lap. "I've just never met anyone like you before. Do you think—I'm sorry, just, do you think I could see? Do you have scars?" You clear your throat, feeling confined. She relaxes her face a little. "I thought this was your homework assignment."

You try to see what her game is, but there's only genuine curiosity in her eyes—and it isn't pity. You know pity. You've seen it in Isaac's face too many times to count. Her fingers move to yours again. "Okay. Just don't freak out." You pull your sleeve to your elbows and show her the one long scar following the veins in your wrist and the recent slice across it from your birthday.

"Okay, you saw it." You pull your sleeve back down.

"John," she says, half smiling. "That was amazing."

"You're fucking crazy." You stand up so you can look away from her, but she stands too.

"How do you do it?" she asks.

"What do you mean?"

"I mean, like, usually. What do you use?"

"Why does this interest you so much? It's not cool or amazing. It's fucked up."

She looks hurt and you soften. "I'm sorry. Look.

Here." You open up your pocket knife. You've cleaned it and haven't used it since you started the support group. Haven't even opened it until now, but for some reason you couldn't give up taking it out of your pocket. You turn the handle, watching the blur of her ceiling light in the metal. The edge looks sharper than you remember it. It would probably be the perfect cut—it might not even leave a scar.

She takes it out of your hands, even though you suddenly don't want to let go of it. "So, like . . . " She puts the blade on her wrist.

"Holy shit, stop." You grab it out of her hand. "You don't cut the veins in your wrist, you'll bleed out. You're not trying to kill yourself."

"What are you trying to do?"

"I don't know," you sigh. You can't seem to close the blade again. "Forget, maybe? I don't know. It doesn't matter the reason, it's just—" You close your eyes so that you can't see the blade and recite, "Harmful physically, emotionally, mentally, and socially."

"That from your class?" she asks.

"Yup."

You both are silent for a while, and then she says, "You only have, like, two scars. How long have you been going to this thing?"

"I don't only have two." You start playing with the knife, flipping it around in your hand. The weight of it is familiar, nostalgic. You look back up at her and see how intensely she's watching you, like she's scared and excited at the same time. Reluctantly, you toss the knife on the bed and unzip your jacket. When you pull your shirt over your head, she grabs your arm and gasps.

"I feel like there is so much more to you than what's on the surface," she finally says, after tracing her fingers along the scars on your shoulder—all the half-moons and lightning bolts and nicks and crosshatches. "You're just so much deeper than other guys. You know?"

You don't know how to answer her and she keeps touching you, circling around your back and touching the scars on your other shoulder. Suddenly she gets lower, trailing her hands down.

"I've always liked you," she says. She unbuttons your pants and pulls them down. "Oh," she says, not unhappy when she sees you have scars on your thighs. "I've never been with a cutter before." She starts to put her mouth on you and you grab her hair. She looks up when you don't seem to be responding. "What? Am I doing something wrong?"

There are so many things going through your head you don't even know what to say. You shake your head and let go of her. She keeps moving back and forth. You finally get it up when you think about Isaac. Even now, that motherfucker won't get out of your head. You have to stop yourself from saying his name. You keep your eyes closed.

When you finally climax, you find your eyes burning and you rub the tear off your cheek before it falls.

She sits on the edge of the bed and combs through her hair with her fingers. You sit next to her and grab the knife, still open. You don't hesitate.

You can't think, you just need to feel it, the metal, so you can stop thinking his name.

She holds your wrist while you do a quick cut on your thigh. "John, you're not supposed to do that. You're going to a support group."

"I don't care," you say, but really you want to tell her to shut up. You need this. You focus on the sting coming off the blade, the red coming up through your skin from underneath. Suddenly she has her arms on either side of you and kisses you on the mouth. With some effort you pull your focus back to her.

"It's okay, John," she says between breaths. "I'll take care of you."

You decide that you'll let her help you be who you want to be. Who your parents want you to be. It's supposed to feel unnatural at first. It's only been a few days of holding her hand during school and kissing her after class before you're back at support group. You don't tell them that you're cutting again, though they give you a round of applause for

185

opening up to someone outside of the group. You almost tear up in front of them because you suddenly want to dig the knife in until you bleed to death.

The next day at school, Sofia holds your hand between classes. She kisses you when she first sees you, right in the middle of saying hello, before class. This is good. More kissing means more progress, more redemption.

"So, we are together now, right?" she asks at lunch. "We never actually said it out loud."

So it's like everything else in this place—once it's said out loud it's true. Typical. Before you can answer, you hear a shout from behind the cafeteria. A few freshmen run past you.

"Sounds like a fight," Sofia says, raising her eyebrows. She pulls your hand to follow. When you turn the corner of the cafeteria you have to stop yourself from letting go of her and running over to him. Isaac has someone tackled to the ground and he's punching him in the face over and over. When you see the other guy, you recognize Lenny, Lucy's friend from the wrestling team.

Sofia turns to someone next to her. "Al, what's this about?"

"Lenny called Isaac a *maricon*," he says, trying to look around the crowd to see better. He laughs. "He sure doesn't like that."

Isaac suddenly flips and lands on his back. It seems to knock the wind out of him and he starts wheezing and coughing. He tries to turn on his belly but Lenny straddles him and punches him across the jaw. He lifts him up partway by his shirt and then punches him again, letting his head hit the cement.

"Someone should stop him," you say. Isaac is pulling on Lenny's shirt helplessly, but he hits him harder.

Al looks at you suspiciously and gestures to your hand holding Sofia's before turning back to the fight. "You guys together now or what? You know I heard from Lenny—well, never mind."

"What? What has Lenny been saying?"

Sofia looks up at you and raises her eyebrows.

"Just that you and Isaac were hanging out pretty late at the park. But now—" Al shrugs at your hand holding Sofia's. You guess it really is this easy.

You look back at the fight, but there are too many people in front of you to see. Just a few flashes of Isaac's hair, his black hoodie. "I have to stop this," you say, but you're not even sure how you would. "You'd think a fucking teacher would be around, you know?"

"Look out, Sofia," Al says, turning back to the fight. You ignore the suspicious look she gives you and let go of her hand.

So Isaac never ratted you out, which means you abandoned him for all the wrong reasons. You're not about to abandon him again.

To help Isaac yourself, turn to page 189.

To find a teacher to help, turn to page 199.

# 16

Lenny is still pummeling Isaac in the face when you rush into the crowd toward the fight. Sofia shouts after you, "What are you doing?"

You push past the crowd and into the inner circle. "Get off of him!" You grab Lenny by the back of the shirt, but he shoves you off, still concentrated on Isaac. You drive both hands into his shoulder hard enough to make him fall down beside Isaac. The crowd yells louder, drowning out Sofia.

You're standing over them both: Isaac wiping the blood from under his nose and Lenny heaving himself back up. He lunges toward you and tackles you to the ground, making your legs bend painfully under him. He's too heavy to move so you cover your face with your forearms and try to breathe again. The crowd yells for someone to make a move.

"What's your deal, fag?" He tries to move your arms to punch you in the face but you manage to keep them there, grabbing the back of your head for support. "Miss your boyfriend?"

"Leave him alone," Isaac says, panting. From between your arms, you see Lenny look back at him over his shoulder. Isaac's hunched over like it would hurt to stand up straight. He wipes his face when blood leaks out of his nostrils.

You throw yourself upright and into Lenny's shoulder, knocking him on his back. The two of you roll over to your side. Suddenly Isaac's with you. He pins down Lenny's arm with his leg to hit him and he does, hard. It makes a cracking noise that must have been his nose. You grab Lenny's other arm and drag him back. Isaac helps you lift him up. He yells, "Truce! Truce! Fuck. You broke my nose." He spits blood on the ground. "Fuckers. Broke my nose!"

Isaac punches him in the stomach while you brace to hold Lenny up. He blows out a breath that sounds like it chokes him but you keep him standing. "Fuck!" he yells, wincing.

Then it's like the crowd gets closer, like they decided enough was enough. You drop him at the same time Isaac gets a final hard punch to the side of Lenny's face and he slumps to the ground, head cracking on the concrete. You know Isaac needed that. The crowd roars up around you, a mix of cheering and cussing, but mostly shock. You look up at Sofia walking past Isaac. She drops her hands from her mouth and grins.

"Holy shit, John." You heart is still pumping as you walk around her to Isaac, looking at his blond, greasy hair hanging in his eyes. You haven't done anything but lie since you decided to bring him to your birthday dinner. This time he's not stopping you. He doesn't know what's best for you. You do.

"Hey—" he starts but it gets muffled. You kiss him hard on the mouth, tasting the blood in his teeth. When you pull away, he looks at you wide-eyed for just a second before closing his eyes and kissing you back. You listen to people cheering, people booing, people disgusted. He was looking out for you since the beginning. This is where you belong, right in the middle of the gritty, bloody truth.

---

You only get a few weeks of detention considering that Lenny started the fight with a homophobic slur. Some people at school still won't look either of you in the eye, but that doesn't stop you from meeting in public. You still go to the park every week because, well, it's tradition.

It's around midnight and Isaac sits on a tree that fell in your spot. He watches you walk up to him.

"The group knows about me now. They brought it up today in session." You step up on the log and back down. "A few of them don't talk to me anymore, but I'm okay. They need the group whether I'm there or not. Whether I'm gay or not."

Isaac kicks at the dirt. "You still cutting?" You're silent for a while and Isaac just shakes his head. At least you haven't been cutting as often. When you do, it's mechanical, a habit. "Your parents don't know about us?" he says.

"Nope." You grab your wrist in your hand and squeeze. You lean over and kiss him, relieved that you can. But he pulls back, grabbing the hand that you have latched on your wrist and he laces his fingers in yours.

"You can't blame yourself. You can't live your whole life thinking that everything that ever goes wrong is because of the fact that you're gay. It's like you think that's all there is to you anymore."

"I don't know what world you live in, Isaac, but that's the only reason everything went to shit."

He looks tired. "You're not just one thing, John, and that's okay. You believe in God, that's part of who you are. Your parents didn't love what they thought was your heterosexuality before, they loved their son. And you love them even if they reject you—that's who you are. You love me too." He doesn't say anything for a while. "Tell your family. It's only a matter of time."

"I think you're overestimating how easy talking to my family is. Your family's cool about it. I promise you, mine's not."

"Well, just think about it, okay? Keep trying."

You're about to fight him on it, but you know that look. Besides, he's right. The only way to stop is to start working on it. On your way home, you think about your future, everything that you know about yourself now and what you know you want to accomplish. You think about the rest of your life, how long it could be, how full it could be, before tossing your knife into a dumpster and walking away.

After your last class the next day, you borrow some money from Isaac to take a bus to your *abuelita*'s house. When she opens the door, she immediately pulls you in for a hug. "I was wondering if you'd ever show up, *nieto*."

She tells you in Spanish slow enough for you to understand, that you're always welcome to stay with her as long as you need. "You were smart to come to me. Your parents won't understand."

You look at her gray eyes, wondering if you should ask her what she means, since you've decided that part of your new philosophy is making sure to speak up. "You *know?*"

"I was at the dinner," she says, giving you another hug. You look away, wanting to forget that night forever.

"I didn't think anyone in this town would help me."

"Looks like the town isn't the only one putting people in boxes." She smiles and looks up at the stars. "It is up to God to judge, not me, not your parents, not even you. My job is to protect my family—something your parents don't understand. If anyone does not provide for his own, and especially for those of his household, he has denied the faith, and is worse than an unbeliever. Timothy 5:8."

You let the words sink in. "What did my parents say to you?"

"They said that if you ever admitted what they suspected was true that night, they would need the light of God to save you."

You shiver on her porch and she puts an arm over your shoulder to bring you inside. Like Isaac said, it's only a matter of time before they find out—it doesn't matter. They'd never admit what they know. You're going to live with your *abuelita*, so they can pretend like it isn't true. It's an unspoken agreement, like usual, here. If you don't say it, they won't bring it up.

---

After graduation, you get a job working with a heating and air company. It pays, but by the time you can afford a car, you realize it will be a long time until you can afford college tuition. Isaac is across the country at Penn State, experiencing his first real winter. You talk to each other on the phone as often as you can, but you're both busy most of the time. College is going well for him. His roommates are nice and he got a B+ on his first midterm in his human rights class.

"I want to help people like us," he says. "I want to make a difference."

"I'm sure you will," you say but you stutter. You're trying to pin your nametag on straight. Isaac is making new friends. You keep missing each other's calls. You open your mouth but close it again. He notices anyway, even over the phone. He always does.

"Don't you dare ask," he says. "Don't you dare ask if I'm sure about us."

You breathe deeply, actually smiling. Every once in a while you'll feel it sometimes—the need to be reassured, the need for him to tell you that he still loves you, that he'll still be here, even though sometimes you'll get that old feeling that you don't

197

deserve the love he gives you. But you know yourself now. You threw that knife away because you know you're more than what your brain tells you. You are not just scar tissue.

Still, the words are nice to hear, and you'll see him in a few weeks once fall semester is through.

"I love you, Jay. Even long distance, even with all the shitheads in the world—"

"I know. *Te amo*, Isaac. Always." Your voice feels strong again. You look at your nametag. It says, John "Juan" Carlos Garcia. "We're worth it."

The End

# 17

YOU RUN IN THE OPPOSITE DIRECTION, SHOVING PAST PEOPLE AND turning through hallways until you get to the main office.

"There's a fight. Hurry." You lead a few startled adults toward the gym, trying to make them move faster but they do a light jog the whole way—two women and a man you don't recognize. "There." You point to the crowd, now hunched down, not moving or cheering, just looking.

You run ahead of them. Isaac is on the ground, eyes closed tight, holding his stomach. Everyone leans over him, talking to each other, mostly. No one's even worried about how he's doing. You shove them out of the way and put your hand on his chest.

"Hey, you okay? Wake up." He groans but doesn't open his eyes.

The teachers tell everyone to back off and they give them space. "You, too," the man says. You watch them try to coax him to his feet but he won't. He can't. They decide to call for an ambulance.

You shove Sofia off when she grabs your arm.

"It's just a fight, calm down. You don't even know that guy." She pulls you away from the group that has started closing in again until you can't see him anymore. "Come on."

You make yourself look at her. Besides Isaac, she's the only one in this whole fucking town that's ever given a damn about you. She's everything you were trying to build to. If you stay, you're the one who's going to be on the ground next week, and then the next, for the rest of your life.

When she pulls you far enough away she puts a

hand on your cheek. "Jeez, you look really worked up."

"I'm fine." You lean in to kiss her and the fact that she doesn't hesitate at all, that no one looks twice when you do it or cusses you out or shoves you away, makes you never want to stop. You have to stay safe. Isaac made his sacrifice for you—kept your secret so you wouldn't have to deal with what he deals with. You have to honor that.

When he doesn't show up at school the next day, you find out that he's in the hospital with a broken nose and two broken ribs. He's in recovery.

You skip sixth period to see him. You tell Sofia you forgot a textbook at home and she kisses you goodbye.

"Dinner with your family tonight?" she asks.

You nod. She's meeting your parents for the first time. They're going to love her.

On the bus, you try to think of something to say but nothing feels adequate to explain how grateful you are for what he did for you—the sacrifices he's making every day. You feel like you need to apologize but you're not sure for what.

Still, he has to see that you care enough to visit—that's something.

You finally make it through small talk with the hospital staff and get them to show you to his room, but you hesitate outside the door before walking in. Isaac is sitting up in bed with bandages wrapped over his nose. He has the remote in one hand and is watching the TV that pulls out over the bed. He looks mad and clicks the button over and over. Then he pushes the TV off to the side but it looks like it hurts and he winces as he touches his chest. When he opens his eyes he sees you.

"Hey, man," you say and walk in.

"I was wondering when you'd show up." He drops the remote on the table next to him.

You hold your wrist. "How are you?"

"I saw you with Sofia," he says. "You know, through the pain of getting the shit kicked out of me while you watched."

"I was the one who got help," you say, trying to keep your voice down. "You should be grateful that I even bothered saving your stupid ass."

"Awesome," he says and grabs the TV to pull it back. You want to shake him, tell him to snap out of it, stop being such an asshole. You walk over and push the TV back before he can turn it on.

"Stop it, okay? I did what I had to do. There's no way I could take on that guy by myself."

"Oh, and I could?" He gestures to his blue hospital gown. He has dark circles under his eyes, which are pink like he's been crying.

"I'm sorry." You sit on the bed tentatively as he glares at you. "I'm here now."

"Your denial is really cheering me up."

"What's your problem?"

"My problem is you're going to fuck that girl for a couple of months, maybe even years. Maybe you'll even marry the skank, because you won't accept who you really are. Is this not enough of a wake-up call? Was seeing me bleeding on the fucking ground not enough?" He swallows and it looks like he's tearing up. "I'm the one who had to pick up the pieces of you when you cut too deep. I'm the one with a broken fucking nose and internal bleeding. I'm the one with the family I have to lie to about school. 'Uh, yeah, mom. Everything is fine. I have so many friends who are okay with me being gay,' so they can smile at me. They *smile*. So they can feel like I'm safe. I'm the one who pretends that everyone calling me a faggot all the time or pushing me when I walk down the hall doesn't get to me. I'm the one who has to act strong, not you."

"I think I get it now," you say, standing. "You brought me into your fucked-up head, made me think I'm just as fucked up as you are so you feel less alone. I'm with Sofia, now. Why don't you get that?"

"You love me and you know it."

"You ruin everything! My relationships, my body." You roll up your sleeves and show him the scars.

"Be honest with yourself for once, John!"

"You want honesty? You want to know the real reason I was with you?" You lower your voice, hesitating at the words, terrified of them. "You were the only other gay guy I knew."

You leave before you can look at his face again, not wanting to see what's there.

You have only seen Isaac a few times since he got out of the hospital. Once, a few weeks ago, when Lucy shoved him out of his desk as he sat down for class, you laughed with your new friend, Al, who you met through Sofia. You pretend, sure, but you were always happy it wasn't you. Pretending is what people have to do to survive in this town. You feel guilty but the feeling of self-defense somehow became stronger.

A few days later a group of people stand around him on the quad and you only see him get pushed once before you turn away and hold Sofia's hand tighter. Whether or not it's fixing you, you have to pretend to be straight. All that matters is how it looks.

You keep going to your support group, because it feels like the only sliver of reality you have left, even though you're still cutting. But during today's session, something feels off. At break, Sarah says, "You hear what happened?"

A new member, an older woman nods, "So sad. He was sixteen."

The big guy leans forward, almost yelling, "Can someone explain what's going on?"

"That kid from El Doro High School," Sarah says, rolling her eyes. She holds her cup tighter and adjusts her feet. "Overdosed late last night. I guess everyone was making fun of him at school for being gay. He just couldn't take it anymore."

You freeze.

"It's a shame. All the people that cared about him will never be the same because of one impulsive decision. I wish he could have found the group first," José says.

"Who?" you finally ask. Everyone turns to you and you ask again. "Who was it? What was his name?"

"Oh yeah, you go to that school, don't you? It was some guy . . . I think his name started with a vowel?"

"I—Isaiah? Something like that?"

"Yeah, I think that was it."

You stand up. José puts his hand toward you to sit back down. "Are you okay, John? Did you know him?"

"No. I mean, yes. My girlfriend knows him," you say. You make yourself sit again.

"She's hot," the big guy says.

"We're so sorry." Sarah puts her hand on yours. "It must be tough for her."

You look around at everybody staring at you, waiting for you to say something. "I didn't know him. From what I hear, he was an asshole anyway."

Some look away and go silent. Sarah lets go of your hand.

"Everyone has their side of the story. You never know what kind of sacrifices a person is making day to day just to survive, right under your nose," José says, looking only at you. "Let yesterday's tragedy be a lesson to all of you about the importance of appreciating each other and appreciating yourself—your virtues and your faults. The word I want you to remember is empathy. Learn to appreciate the struggle of another, and you will learn to appreciate your own."

"His name is Isaac," you say, trying not to cry.

After a short silence, he nods, slightly confused. "To Isaac." He raises his cup and the others follow.

"To Isaac."

The End